Clara's World
San Francisco in 1906

Cliff House

Seal Rocks

Clara's yard

Clara's house

Golden Gate Park

Tent city

Ocean Beach

THE STRANGE CASE
OF BABY H

❧

by
Kathryn Reiss

Visit our Web site at **americangirl.com**

Printed in the United States of America.
02 03 04 05 06 07 RRD 10 9 8 7 6 5 4 3 2 1

History Mysteries® and American Girl®
are registered trademarks of Pleasant Company.

PERMISSIONS & PICTURE CREDITS
The following individuals and organizations have generously given permission to reprint
illustrations contained in "A Peek into the Past": p. 157—painting by unknown artist, 1906;
pp. 158–159—rubble-filled street, © CORBIS; newspaper page, Library of Congress; poster,
Californiana Collection, San Jose Public Library; girls in tent city, © Underwood &
Underwood/CORBIS; relief worker, California Historical Society, FN-32650 (detail); houses,
© Bettmann/CORBIS; pp. 160–161—cooking outside, Fine Arts Museums of San Francisco,
Museum Purchase from the Estate of Arnold Genthe, James D. Phelan Bequest Fund, A046260;
tent classroom, Californiana Collection, San Jose Public Library; Caruso, © Bettmann/CORBIS;
Cliff House, Marilyn Blaisdell Collection; pp. 162–163—Sutro Baths, Marilyn Blaisdell
Collection; bathing suit, Paul Johnson Picture Collection; seal, © Paul A. Souders/CORBIS;
San Francisco skyline, Getty Images/FPG.

Cover and Map Illustrations: Douglas Fryer
Line Art: Greg Dearth

Library of Congress Cataloging-in-Publication Data

Reiss, Kathryn.
The Strange Case of Baby H / by Kathryn Reiss. — 1st ed.
p. cm. — (History mysteries ; 18)
"American girl."
Summary: In the aftermath of the 1906 San Francisco earthquake,
twelve-year-old Clara finds a baby left on the doorstep of her family's boarding house,
and sets out to unravel the surrounding mysteries.

ISBN 1-58485-534-7 — ISBN 1-58485-533-9 (pbk.)
1. Earthquakes—California—San Francisco—Juvenile fiction.
[1. Earthquakes—California—San Francisco—Fiction. 2. Kidnapping—Fiction.
3. Boardinghouses—Fiction. 4. San Francisco (Calif.)—History—20th century—Fiction.
5. Mystery and detective stories.]
I. Title. II. Series.
PZ7.R2776 St 2002   [Fic]—dc21   2001056020

For Helen Curfman Mason,
beloved great-aunt,
and
once again for Tom Strychacz,
my husband, my hero.
You inspire me.

TABLE OF CONTENTS

Chapter I
EARTHQUAKE!

Clara streaked through the waves like a sleek gray seal. "I'm coming!" she cried to the figure struggling in the water. "Hang on, Old Sock!" She dragged him up onto the sun-baked rocks and pulled herself out after him. She lifted her mouth to breathe in the salty sea air—and got a mouthful of . . . thick fur?

With a start, twelve-year-old Clara Curfman awoke from another swimming dream to find her big sheepdog shoving his furry face into hers. In the next second he had leaped up onto her bed—heedless of Mother's rule against Dogs On Beds—and was burrowing beneath the blankets.

"Botheration!" groaned Clara. "What *are* you doing, Humphrey?"

Mother would never allow such a thing, but Clara slid over to make room for Humphrey. The dog lay at her side, panting heavily.

Clara closed her eyes. The dream hovered in her mind,

but the yowling cats and howling dogs outside her window made sleep impossible. Humphrey pawed the bedclothes. He seemed to be trying to hide. "What's *wrong*, boy?" Clara hissed, struggling to sit up.

She listened with surprise to Mr. Grant's rooster crowing next door. *It's still dark!* Clara thought in protest. *Don't these silly animals know it's the middle of the night?*

But the palest dawn light filtering through the windows illuminated the clock on Clara's dresser: eleven minutes past five. Almost time for the usual six o'clock rising.

The very thought of morning made Clara close her eyes again. Another day of chores, chores, chores—and then more chores. Another day of *Mother.* Clara wished she could go back to sleep for a million years, but her eyes flew open when her bed lurched like something alive and Humphrey growled.

The room jolted as if shaken by a giant's hand. Humphrey's frantic barking merged with crashes and thuds from all around the house as everything shook violently from side to side and up and down.

Hang on, Old Sock! Her brother's voice rang in Clara's head as she clutched Humphrey in panic. She couldn't think what was happening. She heard church bells clanging wildly, shouting from somewhere very far away—and Mother's shrill voice screaming, "Earthquaaaaaaaake!"

Clara twined her fingers tight in Humphrey's long fur as the floor heaved like rolling ocean waves. She watched in amazed horror as her books jiggled right off the shelves by the bed. They cascaded onto her and Humphrey, sharp corners gouging them through the blankets. Clara tried to jump out of bed—but Humphrey was on top of her, howling. Plaster came raining down on them from the ceiling, and in some part of her mind Clara knew she must take cover— perhaps under the bed? But she just couldn't move.

The shaking and heaving went on and on, the bed cresting the waves. And then it started dancing right across the sunporch floor with Clara a frozen passenger, unable to stop it. The bed smashed into the far wall. Window glass shattered over the foot of the iron bedstead, and puffs of plaster flew like sharp grains of sand into Clara's face.

Then—for one long moment—all was silent.

In the silence Clara thought dizzily: *I liked the swimming dream better* . . . but Humphrey licked her face and she knew this chaos was no dream. As she brought her hands to her face and wiped off the gritty plaster dust, she heard her mother's voice crying her name.

"Clara! My Clara!"

Clara struggled out of her cocoon of covers, shoving Humphrey onto the floor. "Mother!" She jumped down from her bed and felt something sharp stab her heel. "Ow!"

Mother was a dim figure in the doorway, her long brown hair out of its usual tidy bun and coated with white dust. "Oh, my heavens, take care, child! Watch for the broken glass, darling—"

She called me darling! Even through her fear, Clara felt astonished at Mother's endearment. Mother usually had nothing but critical remarks for Clara.

"Hurry, hurry!" Mother clutched Clara's arm as Clara bent to ease the sliver of glass from her foot. "We must hurry outside. There may be more in store—oh, my land, the house could crumble around our heads and bury us all alive!"

Mother led the way from the sunporch, her tall, thin figure whisking around the corner as Clara limped along more slowly, her heel throbbing with pain. *I'm probably leaving bloody footprints on the carpet runner,* she thought. *Mother will have a dozen fits . . .* They hurried down the long staircase to the front door. Clara gasped as they passed the parlor. It looked as if a storm had swept through, tossing furnishings about like loose pages of newspaper on the street. The mirror over the mantle had shattered, and so had the clock. Shards of silvered glass lay on the mahogany bench.

The lodgers appeared in the front hallway in their nightshirts, looking like ghosts. Old Mr. Granger had on a nightcap—*the ghost of Wee Willy Winky,* Clara thought wildly. She felt dizzy and light-headed as the nervous lodgers gathered around her. Mother shooed everyone toward the front door.

"Where is Father?" Clara demanded. It should be Father in command, not Mother. In her mind's eye, she saw how he would leap over the wreckage and lead the way out of the house with old Mr. Granger slung over his shoulder and one of the ladies under each arm . . . But that was impossible now.

"Mind the glass," Mother warned Miss Abigail Chandler, the young piano teacher who now slept in Clara's old bedroom. "Clara! Do hurry!"

"Where is Father?" Clara grabbed Mother's arm.

"I'll come back for him once I get you all safely outdoors."

"I'll get him myself!" cried Clara, and she turned and hobbled, heel throbbing, through the dining room, where broken china littered the floor, toward the small study where her parents had been sleeping.

"No, Clara! You must leave the house at once!" shouted Mother. But Clara ran faster.

She found Father sitting on the edge of his bed, clutching the iron bedpost. He was trying to pull himself up to a standing position. "My Clara," he spoke quietly when he saw her in the doorway. "I trust you are unhurt?"

She limped over to him. "Yes, Father." She could hear her own heartbeat pumping in her head. The noise felt like a drumbeat to get them marching: *Get out quickly! Get out of the house!*

"But you're bleeding, my girl."

"I stepped on glass, that's all," she replied, trying to speak just as calmly as he did. "Hurry, Father. Mother says we must get out into the yard before—" She broke off as another jolt shook the house. Father fell back onto the bed. Clara grabbed hold of the dresser and reached out to intercept the wicker wheelchair as it careened toward them from the far side of the room.

The house trembled as if shaken by the scruff of its neck. Then it dropped—down, down—and Clara's stomach lurched down with it. More plaster sifted around them, covering their identical auburn heads like snow and frosting Father's beard. Clara shook back her tangled, waist-long hair.

"Snow in San Francisco," grunted Father.

"Is it over now?" whispered Clara. Then they heard Mother shouting for them, her voice rising hysterically. Clara grabbed the wheelchair and pulled it over to the bedside. Father eased himself into the seat, and she took hold of the wooden handles.

They hastened into the back hallway. Out on the stoop, Clara was relieved to see that the wooden ramp for Father's wheelchair was intact. Clara blinked in the half-light and sucked in a deep breath of early-morning air as she and her father reached the grass. Mr. Hiram Stokes, a middle-aged office clerk, came running around the house from the front and took charge of the wheelchair; Mother was right behind him, and she wrapped her shawl around Clara's shoulders. The other lodgers straggled after Mother into the small backyard. Humphrey pressed his wet nose into Clara's hand as she gazed at the unusual sight of the lodgers in their nightclothes and curling rags, nightcaps and bare feet. She stroked Humphrey's head.

"You knew it was coming, didn't you, boy? That's what all your fussing was about. Somehow you knew."

Humphrey thumped his tail, and Clara's shuddering heart slowed to nearly normal. She looked around at the twisted iron fence, the broken glass, the mess. But at least her family and all the lodgers were out of the house unhurt—the only injury was Clara's foot, and that was a trifling matter compared to what could have happened—and the house still stood whole, except for the windows.

Thanks be to God—they were safe!

No sooner had Clara thought this than Humphrey pressed against her side, whining, and the ground beneath their feet tossed them forward. Clara landed on her knees, wincing. She gripped the arm of Father's wheelchair with both hands to pull herself up again.

"Merciful heavens!"

"Lord save us!"

"Watch out!"

From all around the neighborhood came the sounds of people shouting, someone's high-pitched screaming, thudding bricks, and cracking boards. The Curfman family and their five lodgers clustered together. *Safety in numbers,* Clara thought, pressing against Mother. Geoffrey Midgard wrapped his burly arms around Miss Chandler and Miss Peggy DuBois, the violin teacher. Hiram Stokes gripped old Mr. Granger's shoulder. Father's head was bowed as he sat in his wicker chair. It looked to Clara as if Father were praying.

But of course Father never prayed anymore.

Clara's heart was thumping wildly again, and the glimmer of safety she'd felt only moments ago was gone now. Mother walked out to the street, calling to neighbors, asking if anyone needed help. The closely spaced houses along Clara's street were still standing, but Clara saw that their own house's chimneys and those of the house next door had collapsed into piles of brick. Jagged shimmers of glass littered the yard near the house. The Curfmans' house seemed otherwise intact, but how could they ever be sure it would be safe to go inside again? Where would they ever be safe if even the earth they stood upon couldn't be trusted?

In the distance they heard the clang of alarm bells, and Father lifted his bowed head. "There's fire," he pronounced in his gravelly voice.

Now Clara could see plumes of smoke rising into the dawn sky. Fire, she knew, could sweep a city. Her whole world was falling to pieces, and she reached down to Humphrey for comfort. He was trembling.

Nobody was safe, she realized. Nobody, and nowhere. Her eyes stung with unshed tears and smoke. Her heel throbbed. And miles beneath her feet, the earth started rumbling again.

CHAPTER 2

THE WORLD TURNED
UPSIDE DOWN

Clara braced herself, arms around Humphrey, until the trembling stopped.

"More and more quakes!" Miss DuBois moaned. "I can't bear it!"

"We're all right," Miss Chandler comforted her. "Everything will be all right."

Clara shivered in the early-morning air. The dawn sky was striped now with columns of smoke. Miss Chandler was trying to be kind and brave, but everything most certainly was *not* going to be all right. *We could so easily have been killed,* Clara thought. *We weren't, but surely others were . . .* She breathed in the sooty smell of burning. *Or will be . . .*

The clang of alarm bells in the distance made Clara wince. Mother beckoned to her. "People will be homeless," Mother said in a dazed voice. "Or hurt. I need you to help me make ready for them."

"But where will we put people?" asked Clara. "We're not a hospital!"

"We are uninjured," said Mother more firmly. "We seem to have escaped the worst, and so of course we will help others as we can."

"Fire's going to spread fast," Father intoned from his wheelchair. "If the wind picks up, we may not remain so fortunate."

"There you go," snapped Mother. "Still the sea captain, are you? Reading the winds?" She turned away, linking her arm through Clara's. "Let's find something to bandage up your foot, dear, and then you shall be my chief helper."

Mother climbed up the ramp into the house and Clara followed morosely. San Francisco might burn to the ground, but still Mother would find chores for Clara to do. The whole state of California might be shaken off the map, but chores would never perish. Clara looked around the wreckage of their kitchen and sighed. Broken crockery lay on the floor. Tins of flour, sugar, and salt had tipped off the counter, their contents muddied on the floor by spilled coffee beans and oil.

"There's no water," Mother announced, trying the taps at the iron sink. "We'll swab you with vinegar, Clara. Come here."

Clara bit her lip at the sting as Mother cleaned her heel. Then Mother ripped a strip off a clean dishtowel to wrap tightly around the injured foot. "Better now?"

Mother reached for the broom that had fallen under the table. "Now you can start sweeping up in here while I go find your shoes and a dress. And a ribbon to tie back your hair . . ." Mother turned to leave, muttering under her breath. "And we'll get a fire going in the stove. People are going to need breakfast after this shock."

Clara gripped the broom handle. She could see she'd be trapped cleaning all day. But what about Emmeline's birthday party tomorrow? It had been so hard to get Mother's permission to go to the party, and so unfair if the quake should ruin everything!

Since turning their home into a boardinghouse, Mother had kept Clara so busy that there was rarely ever time for fun. No afternoons with Emmeline, Clara's dearest friend. No time to visit the library as Clara used to do every week. And certainly no time for swimming . . . *Certainly* not swimming. Never again.

Since the accident, there was little money. Father could no longer work, and the lodgers' fees went for groceries and other necessities. Father and Mother had once talked eagerly about college educations for their children, and going to college was one of Clara's fondest dreams, though Gideon had said he'd rather be a steamship pilot and didn't need a college degree. But now college was not an option for Gideon and was unaffordable, anyway, for Clara. "Out of the question," Mother said.

Since the accident, Mother *always* said no. Anything

Clara wanted to do was either *dangerous* or *frivolous*. Mother was so unreasonable! And Father—since the accident—wouldn't even listen to Clara's side. "Mother knows best," Father always mumbled when Clara turned to him. Then Mother would hasten Clara onto a new chore, or one of the lodgers would ask her to do some mending. Lodgers were nearly as bothersome as parents.

It wasn't that Clara actively disliked the lodgers— not exactly. Mr. Midgard and Mr. Stokes were passably pleasant; the two music teachers were even friendly. Old Mr. Granger stayed in his room a good deal of the time. But she had found sharing her house these past two years quite disagreeable. Their pretty yellow and white house was meant to be a family home, she felt—not a *hotel*. It felt too small with so many people living in it. The dining room, where Clara served every meal, felt especially cramped with five extra people around the table. One chair was always empty, of course.

What would Gideon be doing if he were here? Clara wondered as she started sweeping the crockery into a pile. Her brother would probably be hurrying around the neighborhood, checking on the safety of their neighbors. Clara decided she would go over to Emmeline's house. No matter that there could be no party; she would still take Emmeline her birthday present. She knew Emmeline would love the little velvet pocketbook Clara had sewn herself.

"When you finish in here," said Mother, coming back

into the kitchen with Clara's clothes, "you can start in the dining room. All that china—smashed! Such a waste—" She broke off with a gasp as a volley of explosions boomed in the distance and the floor shook. Hiram Stokes burst through the swinging kitchen door.

"Stop, Mrs. Curfman! Don't light a fire in the stove!" he yelled.

"Mr. Stokes!" cried Mother.

"The stove, ma'am—have you lit it?"

"No," replied Mother. "I haven't found anything to cook yet—but why?"

He ushered Mother and Clara down the ramp to where Father sat in his wheelchair. Clara's heel throbbed under its bandage. All the lodgers were talking in worried voices, and Miss DuBois was sobbing.

"Gas lines are exploding," Father spoke up into the clamor. "Fire's spreading fast. The whole city could go." He wheeled his chair over to Mother. "You mustn't light the lamps or cook anything in the house, Alice, till the gas lines are repaired. Just a spark—and the next explosion you hear could be *us*."

Clara looked at Father with wide eyes. It was so unlike him these days to speak with authority. He sounded almost like the old Father—the Father before guilt silenced him. Mother also seemed surprised. She regarded him stonily for a long moment.

"Mr. Curfman is right, ma'am," interjected Hiram Stokes.

"I venture to say we'll need permission from the fire marshal before we dare cook indoors."

Mother nodded slowly. "I see," she said. "But then how shall we cook for ourselves? Whatever shall we do?" Her voice rose. "The pantry is a shambles and there's glass everywhere, and what are we to eat?"

"We could build a fireplace from fallen bricks," Clara suggested. "A sort of outdoor grill." She hobbled over and picked up a heavy brick from the pile on the ground.

"Capital idea," said Mr. Stokes, coming to assist her.

"We'll all help," said Geoffrey Midgard, the other middle-aged bank clerk. "In times of trouble, folks pull together."

Miss Chandler and Miss DuBois came forward and started helping Clara carry bricks from the collapsed chimneys onto the patch of grass in the side yard. Mr. Granger, a quilt clutched tightly around his thin shoulders, directed. Mother hurried indoors again to search for breakfast offerings. Father rolled his chair to the side of the house, where he could see their tree-lined street. He stared at the neighbors' brightly painted houses, now with broken steps and chimneys. In the distance, smoke billowed above the rooftops.

Clara was surprised how quickly all of them working together were able to fashion a stove. Two bank clerks, two music teachers, one retired brick mason, and Clara all made a square of brick, several feet high, to hold wood or coal. Father, watching from his chair, directed them to take some of the iron fencing stored in the shed to serve as the grate. It was a crude outdoor grill, but it would work, Clara decided. And Mr. Granger said there might be a way to build an oven, too, if they could find some sort of mortar to hold the brick together . . .

Another boom like cannon fire split the air.

What if Emmeline's family didn't know not to light their stove or lamps? "Mother?" asked Clara. "May I please go check on Emmeline?"

"Not yet, child. We need to get things in order here."

Mother handed out bread and cheese for a hasty breakfast, and they ate beneath the canopy of the oak tree. The sun rose higher in the sky, but the day was unnaturally dark. Frequent explosions in the distance meant new fires were erupting every hour. Mr. Stokes and Mr. Midgard set up boards across two sawhorses to create a table in the side yard. Clara, her mother, and the lodgers all made quick runs into the house to get dressed and to carry foodstuffs and furniture outdoors. Mother brought out a big pot of broth and beans that she had started yesterday and placed it on the makeshift stove, and Miss Chandler and Miss DuBois set themselves the task of chopping cabbage and celery to add to the pot.

Clara didn't feel safe inside the house. She moved quickly, helping to bring out bedding, kerosene lamps, and chairs—things they might need to set up housekeeping in the yard until the house was deemed safe. She worried every time she set foot indoors that another quake would send the walls tumbling down around her.

Clara and Gideon had been born in this house. Clara had played in every room and knew each space intimately. She and her brother had spent years playing out in the small backyard or two blocks away in Golden Gate Park. Mother had trusted Gideon to keep Clara safe and had allowed them the freedom to get new books at the library, to see moving pictures at the cinedrome, and later to take the streetcars all the way across the dunes to the Sutro Baths at Ocean Beach.

Then one day Father had decided to take Gideon with him on a steamship run down the coast, and the accident that changed everything left the steamship wrecked on the rocks, Father badly injured—and Gideon dead.

With Father unable to work anymore, Mother had thrown herself into running a boardinghouse. She and Father moved out of their big bedroom upstairs to sleep instead in the study off the dining room. Now Mr. Midgard and Mr. Stokes shared the master bedroom. Clara moved to the sleeping porch so that the two music teachers could have her sunny bedroom. Old Mr. Granger settled into the guest room. The only bedroom that had no lodger was Gideon's. His room remained just as it had been the day he'd died two years ago—Mother's shrine to her lost boy.

The first weeks after the accident were hazy in Clara's

memory. She remembered only the numbness she'd felt, as if she'd lain too long in the saltwater tank at the Sutro Baths. The water, straight from the Pacific Ocean, was icy cold. A brief plunge could be refreshing—any more and her bones would ache. After Gideon died, Clara ached all over—as if she, not he, had been the one to smash on the rocks where Father's steamship foundered. She had missed Gideon with a sharp intensity at first, but now, two years later, the ache had dulled. She sometimes forgot he was gone; when she heard an amusing story at school or learned a new joke, she'd think, *Wait till I tell Gideon!*— and then remember that she could not tell him anything anymore. Now she met him only in dreams, dreams where he did not drown because she swam out after him and pulled him to safety on the rocks.

"Beds now," Mother was saying as Clara stepped outside again with several lanterns in her hands. "We'll set up pallets under the tree—" She broke off with a gasp as another volley of explosions boomed in the distance and a whole crowd of people burst through the gate into their backyard.

"Heavens above, is no place safe?" cried a woman with two toddlers clutching her skirt.

"Do you have rooms?" demanded the man at her side. "We were told you run a boardinghouse."

Another family pressed close behind them. "We've nowhere to go!" they told Mother.

"No rooms, but lots of space here in the yard," said Mother, and Clara marveled at the calm in her voice. "We are happy to help as we can."

The new arrivals introduced themselves as the Hansen and Grissinger families whose homes on Market Street had collapsed. "Mercifully none of us perished!" cried Mrs. Hansen to Mother. "But all we could save fits into these two wheelbarrows and one pram!"

They had set off with scores of other suddenly home-less people, all looking for shelter and bearing news of the devastation. Chinatown was rubble! The wharf was on fire! Ferries full of newly homeless families were escaping across the bay; tugs and fishing trawlers were being pressed into service to help evacuate the city. Flames were erupting from burst gas mains all through San Francisco's center.

Not one piece of news that Clara heard was good. *This is the good news,* she told herself firmly, looking around. *All the houses on our street are standing.* She and her family could have been killed, but here they were. The cut on her foot was throbbing under Mother's tight bandage, but that was nothing compared to the suffering of the Grissinger and Hansen families. Rumor had it, they said, that Fire Chief Sullivan had been injured in the quake and nobody knew who was in charge now. Rumor had it that the army was taking over the city. Rumor had it that all the banks were burning—and that Charles Crocker himself, head of one of the largest banks, was seen helping his workers toss money into sacks, hoping to hire a boat to take all the money out into the bay until the fires were out.

The Hansen and Grissinger parents relayed the news, but their small children stood silent. Their eyes were wide with shock. They were wrapped in sooty blankets and still wore their nightclothes.

Mother rose to the occasion. She sent Clara into the house for vinegar to wash wounds. Then she sent her back to find skirts and sweaters from their own wardrobes, and Father's old trousers for the men.

"Gideon's wardrobe is full of clothes," Clara reminded her mother boldly as she handed her an armload of dresses.

"Just stay out of there," Mother ordered, frowning. She helped Clara gather the sheets and blankets off the beds. "We haven't water to wash these," Mother said, "but you can at least shake off all the plaster."

Clara hung the sheets on the washing line strung along the back fence. Clouds of plaster dust sifted down onto the ground below.

Mother heated yesterday's coffee for the new arrivals. A pair of elderly sisters appeared—Amelia and Ottilie Wheeler—shaken and dazed. They, too, were given hot coffee. The six Hansen and Grissinger children whined and fretted while Mother and Clara bandaged cuts and scrapes as best they could. Miss Chandler and Miss DuBois doled out the last of the bread and cheese. Soon the fathers of the two families, along with Mr. Stokes and Mr. Midgard, set off through the streets to see how they could be of help. Father sat in his wheelchair at the curb, watching them go. If things were different, Clara knew, Father would be leading them.

In fact, if the accident had never happened, Clara reflected, Father would be out on the water with his steamboat, ferrying people to safety. Father would never sit home while there was work to be done. Gideon, at sixteen, would be helping, too . . .

Wish you were here, Old Sock, she thought, ripping the last clean tea towel into strips for bandages. She blinked her eyes against the clouds of wind-borne ash. The whole world felt upside down.

CHAPTER 3

BLESSING IN DISGUISE

L ate in the afternoon, Clara slipped inside the house and darted upstairs to the sleeping porch. In the doorway, she stopped and stared in dismay at the wreckage. Her clothes, books, and school satchel were on the floor, covered with plaster dust and glass from the broken windows. Her doll, Delilah, had lost her porcelain head. It lay, shattered, by the dresser. Clara's stomach clenched.

Don't be silly, she told herself. *Delilah is only a doll.* But she picked up Delilah's headless body and laid it gently on the dresser top. She found Emmeline's birthday present on the floor, covered with plaster. At least it wasn't breakable, Clara thought, dusting off the velvet pouch.

She'd decided to check on Emmeline even without Mother's permission. She would go quickly so no one would miss her. She hurried the three blocks to Emmeline's

house, skirting piles of brick and stone. The smell of
smoke was everywhere. Along the way, Clara saw families
tending small campfires in their yards and sheltering
under tents of sheets and tablecloths.

But Emmeline's house stood silent. Clara climbed
the steep steps to the front door and knocked. While she
waited for someone to respond, she leaned to the right
to try to look inside the broken bay window.

No one answered her knock. Could they be hurt?
Or had they gone away?

Clara ran around to the alley behind Emmeline's house.
The gate to Emmeline's backyard hung off its hinges.
No one was there. She hesitated, fingering the soft pouch
in her skirt pocket. She would save it for Emmeline, for
surely Emmeline would return—unhurt! She could not
imagine a world without Emmeline in it—though that,
of course, had once been true about Gideon, too. Clara
and Emmeline had been best friends since they were
eight years old. At Emmeline's house they played with
their paper dolls. At Clara's house they played school,
with Clara as the teacher. Clara, who hoped to go to
college and become a real teacher when she grew up,
enjoyed practicing on Emmeline.

Clara bit her lip in worry as she headed home from
Emmeline's. Mother was waiting in front of their house,
ready to scold, but shouts and alarm bells and the crash
of falling masonry interrupted her tirade. Then—most

frightening of all—came the sound of gunshots. As Mother
and Clara hurried into the boardinghouse's backyard,
Hiram Stokes and Geoffrey Midgard returned with stories
of soldiers shooting looters, and of the army ordering
whole rows of homes that had survived the quake to be
evacuated and dynamited to create firebreaks.

Mother turned pale when she heard about the dynamiting. "Are homes in danger here?" she asked Mr. Stokes.

"Wind's blowing the other way," he said. "I think we're
safe enough."

"We have to watch out for looters," Father said.
"Disaster brings out the best in people—and the worst.
Some people will always take advantage of others' mis-
fortunes." He crossed his arms. "I'll stand guard."

He'll sit guard, Clara thought. But she knew Father
would be vigilant, and he would raise a huge cry if anyone
tried to loot homes along their street. She felt safer knowing that Father would be watching.

Mother was stirring up more porridge to supplement
the cabbage and bean soup for their dinners. "There's
no running water in the house," she announced to the
lodgers. "But we do have our two rain barrels."

"Water mains are broken all over the city, ma'am,"
Mr. Midgard informed her. "Here we are—a city fairly
surrounded by water, but not a drop to drink."

"Well, then, we shall have to make the water in the
rain barrels last," Mother replied. "That will mean no

baths." Then she leaned over and murmured something to Father, and Father glanced at the rain barrels standing under the gutters by the back porch. He nodded and looked around at all the lodgers. Clara understood suddenly that Father would be guarding the water barrels as well.

Mother told Clara to take down the sheets and blankets that had been airing all day and fold them to make pallets for their family and guests. Sighing, Clara looked around for the large wicker basket she had left at the side of the house. But it was gone. And, she realized, so was one of the quilts that had been hanging on the line with the sheets. Mother and Father's large green-and-white diamond quilt was there, but her own soft blue one wasn't.

Looters—already? With the yard full of people? Clara looked around at all the lodgers. The Grissingers and the Hansens were talking quietly among themselves. Miss DuBois was urging the children to eat. Miss Chandler was helping Mother refill the bowls of porridge and soup. Old Mr. Granger and the Wheeler sisters sat in the corner by the back fence, on chairs brought from the dining room. From the wild way Mr. Granger was gesturing, Clara knew he was telling a story about his days as a gold miner, long years ago. He told these tales to anyone who would listen, and Clara had listened many times. She was glad he had a new audience.

.

But no one had her blue quilt.

Clara frowned. There was a wind—it had been whipping up the fires all over the city all day—so perhaps the basket had blown out toward the street. But the quilt? She had pegged it firmly onto the washing line before she'd set off for Emmeline's.

Clara rounded the house, looking in the bushes for the laundry basket. She walked out to the street, with its broken paving stones. She saw the glow of her neighbors' small cookfires.

But no sign of basket or quilt.

Clara shrugged and headed back to the yard. Then she heard a mewling cry. She stopped and listened. There—it came again—from the steep steps leading to their front door.

A lost kitten?

Clara headed for the steps, then stopped. No sign of a kitten—but there, a flash of blue. And—yes—there, set just outside the front door, was the wicker basket with the quilt folded inside.

How odd! Clara thought.

There was the mewling cry again, louder this time. Clara sucked in her breath. She leaped up the steps two at a time.

It wasn't a kitten, not at all! There in the basket, wrapped snugly in the missing blue quilt, was a red-faced, wide-eyed, soot-smudged little baby.

"Oh, gracious!" Clara bent over the basket to read the note pinned to the quilt.

PLEASE TAKE CARE OF ME
FOR I AM A POOR ORFFIN

She looked left and right and across the street to see who could have brought the baby. But no one was there.

Clara lifted the baby into her arms, blue quilt and all. "You're a fine fellow!" she murmured, turning back one corner of the blanket to reveal the baby's grimy blue sailor suit topped by a too-large, torn flannel shirt.

He stared at her. His eyes were dark under his sooty eyebrows and long lashes. He opened his mouth and let out a long, sad wail.

"Oh, dear." She laid him back into the wicker basket, hefted baby and basket together by the wicker handles, and fairly ran into the backyard. "Mother! Father!" she called. "We have another lodger tonight!"

Father was slicing pieces of day-old cake for Mother to distribute as dessert. They turned to Clara as she hurried up to them.

"Oh, good," said Mother. "You've got the laundry down—" Her eyes widened.

"I found him on our doorstep," Clara explained. "Mother, someone just left him there!" She handed her mother the note. "Left him all alone!"

The two young mothers held out their hands, but

Mother lifted the baby out of the basket and cradled him against her shoulder. "What a precious little lad. About five or six months old, I should guess. Wouldn't you agree, ladies?"

The other women nodded. The men looked bemused.

"I do declare," Mother exclaimed. "He is the very image of our Gideon at the same age, don't you think so, Frederick? No hair to speak of—and look at those dark eyebrows!" She handed him down to Father in his wheelchair. Father frowned at the bundle in his lap and patted it awkwardly.

The baby let out a shrill cry.

"Noisy little fellow, and grimy as all get-out," Father remarked. "Been out in the soot and rubble."

"Perhaps his parents were victims of the fire," murmured Miss DuBois. "Poor darling."

"No doubt someone who knows what a fine boarding establishment Mrs. Curfman runs left him for you to find," said Geoffrey Midgard gallantly.

"But why not just bring him to us in person?" Clara asked, frowning. "It seems strange."

"I don't think it's strange at all," Mother replied, lifting the baby back into her arms and cuddling him close. "The Lord moves in mysterious ways, my girl. Here we are, lacking a son. And here is this lad, lacking parents. And him with such a look of Gideon about him! It's fair amazing, that's what it is. Frederick, don't you agree?" She appealed again to Father. "It's Providence, that's what it is."

Father grunted. He reached out and took a slice of cake.

Mother reached out a finger and traced the baby's cheek. "We will take care of him, of course. People have to help each other out in times of trouble."

"You're a good woman, Mrs. Curfman," said Miss Chandler.

Mother handed the baby over to Clara with a sigh. "Take him indoors and clean him up, best you can, Clara. Find him something clean to wear. But don't stay indoors long. It'll be getting dark soon, and we mustn't light lamps in the house."

Clara climbed the ramp with the baby in her arms. She carried him up to her sunporch and laid him on her bed.

Then she smiled down at the squirming infant. "Can you sit up on your own, little fellow?" She pulled him to a sitting position and steadied him with a hand on his back. He managed alone for a few seconds, then toppled backward onto the pillow with a chortle.

"Well," Clara told him, "I'm glad you can find something to laugh about. Because whatever happened to you today certainly looks to be more terrible than what has happened to us. But don't worry, little one. You've got a home here now."

The baby stared up at her with dark eyes. He had no hair at all, so his dark eyebrows and lashes seemed even more pronounced.

"You'll have dark hair when it finally does begin to grow," she told the baby, running her hand over the bald head—then she paused, perplexed. Instead of smooth skin against her palm, she felt the rasp of bristles.

She sat the baby up and bent closer to examine his head. She noticed a scrape at the back of his neck like the ones Gideon had on his chin when he'd practiced shaving with Father's straight razor. "For goodness sakes!" she exclaimed. "You're not naturally bald at all—someone has shaved your head!" *What a strange thing to do to a little fellow,* she thought.

She unfastened the dirty, poorly fitting sailor suit. The child's flannel diaper was sodden. Clara unpinned the diaper—then stopped. "And you're not even a little fellow!" she cried out in surprise. "You're a bald-headed baby *girl!*"

The baby stared up at her solemnly. Clara stared back at the baby, at the sailor suit and flannel she'd just removed, at the bristly shaven head. She felt a strange little prickle of unease at the back of her neck.

Why would anyone shave a baby girl's head, and dress her in boys' clothing?

It was almost as if . . . as if the baby were *in disguise.*

CHAPTER 4

PIECES OF A PUZZLE

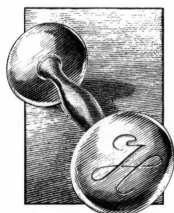

Thoughts in a whirl, Clara tugged open her top dresser drawer and pulled out a soft cotton chemise. Folded, it would work as a diaper for the baby. But what might work as a dress? Her eye fell on Delilah—on Delilah's poor headless body. The doll wore a pretty, flower-sprigged dress that Mother had sewn several years ago. And Delilah was a large doll—bigger than the baby . . .

The dress fit. Clara buttoned it up and smiled with satisfaction. "All right, little lady. You're ready to go back out and meet the lodgers, bald head or no," she murmured. "Likely you'll be wanting something to eat, too." *Do babies this young eat porridge?* she wondered as she reached for the quilt to take along to the yard.

Something fell out of the folds of the quilt and dropped to the floor with a clang. Something else drifted to the floor with a whisper.

Clara reached down to pick up the first thing and found she was holding a silver rattle. The silver was clean and untarnished, gleaming almost white in the dusk of the room. How had a poor baby like this come by such a fancy toy? There was something engraved on the rattle. Clara peered at it closely: a fancy, curlicued letter *H*.

The second thing from the floor was a scrap of paper. On it, oddly, were letters cut from a newspaper, glued together to form words. There were only four words on the scrap Clara held, but the words made her shudder:

SATCHEL TO CLIFF HOUSE

Clara couldn't think what the words might mean, but any mention of Cliff House, that castlelike eight-story building at Ocean Beach near the Sutro Baths, took her breath away. For it was there, on the rocks at the base of Cliff House, that Father's steamship had wrecked in the storm. What could Cliff House have to do with this baby girl?

The baby gurgled—a small growly sound like Humphrey made when he was playing—and reached for the silver rattle. Clara jiggled it, listening to the tinkling bell inside, thinking hard. Such a raggedy baby, dressed in boys' clothes, head shaved—turning out to be a girl. And such an elegant silver rattle, clearly the plaything of a wealthy child. Where had the baby come from? Where, until today, had this baby been living? And with whom? Even if the parents had died in the earthquake or the raging fires, *someone* had brought her to Clara's house, so *someone* must know who she was. That same someone must know what the words on the scrap of paper meant.

Why not just bring the baby right to Mother and ask her to help in this emergency? Why keep the baby's identity a secret? If the clothing and shaven head were meant to disguise—then someone was hiding something.

Could what was being hidden be the baby herself?

A pulse of alarm thudded inside Clara, but she pushed the feeling away. Maybe the scrap of paper was a clue to who the baby really was, and maybe Clara would try to figure it out—but first there were more practical concerns. This baby was hungry, fires were spreading across the city, another quake might come at any moment...it was no time to be standing inside the house playing detective.

"Come on, now, Little H," Clara said to the baby, lifting her from the bed. "You won't be a new son for Mother after all, but let's go show everyone how fetching you look in Delilah's dress."

Outside again, Clara coughed in air full of drifting ash. She could hear shouting in the distance. Kerosene lanterns had been set on the table, their flames flickering in the dusk.

Mother and the lodgers stood talking to a military officer. Clara edged closer, the baby against her shoulder. "What's happening, Mother?"

"He's taking the men to clear the streets of rubble so the fire engines might pass through." Mother shook her head in irritation. "I think most people would help willingly. There's no need for high-handedness!"

Young Mrs. Grissinger, with her two little boys clutching her skirt, clung to her husband. "How long shall he be gone?" she implored the officer. "When shall I see him again?"

"We require the men as long as they're needed, ma'am," replied the officer grimly. "Who can say how long? The fire is spreading fast, and the water mains are broken. People are trapped everywhere, with the fire moving in on them. We have orders to create firebreaks—to stop the fire by any means. You folks here by the park appear to be safe, as long as the wind doesn't change. You are the lucky ones!"

Mrs. Hansen looked to be near tears. "It's nearly dark," she whispered. "Perhaps our men can wait till morning light?"

Her husband patted her hand. "Fires don't mind the dark. And they surely are making enough light to see by. I'll be back soon enough."

The officer cleared his throat impatiently. "Make haste! This is by order of General Funston!"

Mr. Midgard and Mr. Stokes were eager to go. Mr. Hansen and Mr. Grissinger hugged their wives good-bye as if they were marching off to war.

"Who elected *Funston?*" Father inquired from his wheel-chair. "Has Mayor Schmitz declared martial law? Has President Roosevelt?" His mustache trembled.

The officer stared down at Father from his great height. "Perhaps you don't understand the full extent of this disaster, sir. The city is practically destroyed. Troops have been aiding the police and maintaining order. There are thousands of people homeless already, man! And more to be soon if we don't get these men working!" He shoul-dered his rifle. "All right—all you able-bodied men!" He glanced down at Father in his wheelchair. Clara saw Father's shoulders slump. "Let's march!"

Hiram Stokes and Geoffrey Midgard, followed by Mr. Grissinger and Mr. Hansen, marched out of the yard and up the street with the officer. Father glowered after them.

"Oh, do stop looking like a thundercloud, Frederick," snapped Mother. "It does no good—although a real thun-dercloud and plenty of rain would be helpful right now. You know you'd be quick enough to march along with them if you could. You're just in a foul temper!"

Clara hated hearing her parents bickering. She spoke hastily, plunking the baby down on Father's lap. "Look, Mother, Father, we were fooled! This isn't a little boy at all. It's a girl, and look at this—" She held out the silver rattle. "It says 'H'! Why should a girl with a silver rattle be dressed as a raggedy boy? I think it's very strange, don't you?"

Father shrugged. Mother took the rattle and turned it over. "Looks to be fine quality," she agreed. "But strange? I don't think so. I'm sure whoever brought the baby here was fleeing the fires and simply took the first things that came to hand." She picked the baby up out of Father's lap. "Hello, sweeting," she crooned. "We jumped to conclusions, didn't we—seeing how you were wearing boys' clothes and have such a look of our own Gideon about you?" She glanced over at Clara and smiled. "But she has a look of you about her, too, Clara. I see it now. When you were a baby, your lashes were just as long and dark . . . And maybe when her hair grows, it will be red like yours." She turned back to the baby, nuzzling the soft cheek. "We'll take care of you just as if you were our own daughter. That's a promise. And don't you look like a living doll in your new dress!"

Clara felt uneasy. "The baby's head is *shaved*, Mother! Why would somebody do that?"

"I reckon her hair caught on fire after the quake. I daresay someone shaved off the singed bits." Mother turned away with the baby on her shoulder. "Now let's find some supper and make you a bed for the night." And she walked across the yard to Miss Chandler and Miss DuBois as Clara sank down onto a pile of fallen bricks near her father's chair.

"She needs another child again," Father remarked. "Never mind where it comes from or what circumstances bring it. Maybe this catastrophe is a blessing in disguise."

"But I think there's something strange about the baby, Father, don't you? There's no sign of any burn on her head." Clara fished in her skirt pocket. "And there was this. It was folded into the quilt with the rattle." She handed him the scrap of paper.

"Satchel to Cliff House?" He frowned at the words in the flickering lamplight. "Doesn't make sense."

"That's just it," Clara agreed eagerly. "It doesn't make any sense, and look how the letters are all cut from a newspaper and pasted together to make the words. It reminds me of a story we read once in school where a boy was kidnapped, and the kidnappers made a note from newspaper type—just like this—asking for the ransom money to be left in a trunk somewhere . . . and *satchel* reminds me of *trunk* . . ."

Father patted Clara's hand. "Don't let the quake rattle you, daughter," he said wearily. "That baby's not kidnapped. He—*she*—is right here with us, and we'll keep her safe until things settle down. Then we'll decide what to do with her."

"But the note—"

He held up his hand. "Enough. I'm sure it was part of a child's game, interrupted by disaster. Remember, Clara, the quake interrupted many thousands of lives today. Who knows what was going on in any particular home when the earthquake hit this morning?" He opened his fingers, and the scrap of paper fluttered to the ground.

But his offhand question rang in Clara's ears with a sinister echo as she stared over at Baby H, nestled in Mother's arms, sucking porridge off a spoon: *Who knows what was going on when the earthquake hit?* Who knew what was happening to this particular baby? Clara shivered in a gust of smoky wind that sent the little scrap of paper flying across the yard.

She flew after it.

CHAPTER 5

AN AFTERNOON WALK

No one slept well that night. The children fretted and the baby wailed for hours, refusing to be comforted with sips of water from a cup or with spoonfuls of thinned porridge. Clara felt uncomfortable on the hard ground under the oak tree. The air she breathed felt thick and heavy, and roots from the tree poked her in the back. She lay between her parents, listening to the night sounds—the shouting in the distance, the grunting of unfamiliar lodgers nearby, the crooning song Mother sang to the baby—and marveled at how everything could change in an instant.

But then she'd already learned that, hadn't she? Father's boat, strongly built and freshly painted, had been reduced to splintered boards in an instant. And Gideon, champion swimmer on the boy's team at the Sutro Baths, had sunk in an instant and drowned in the cold Pacific.

Miss you, Old Sock, Clara thought sadly, staring into the darkness of the backyard.

Humphrey circled the tree three times, then lay pressed against Clara's feet. Finally, exhausted, they slept.

The morning after the earthquake dawned thick with smoke clouds overhead and the clang of alarm bells. Clara sat up in panic as a thudding boom made the ground tremble.

"It's another quake!" Mother wailed, reaching out for Baby H, who had been nestled for the night in a long dresser drawer.

"The end of the world," murmured Father, lying next to Clara with his eyes still closed. "I'm ready . . . but I'm sorry for my Clara."

"Father!" Clara shook his shoulder. "It's not the end of the world! It's another gas main exploding. Or— I don't know *what* it is!" She covered her ears as another boom, louder than the gas-main explosions, thundered in the distance.

"Sounds like war!" cried old Mr. Granger. He was struggling out of his bedroll over by the back fence. "I remember cannon fire at Gettysburg!"

"No," called Miss Chandler. "Not war—it's dynamite! Remember what the officer told us yesterday. They must be blowing up buildings to create firebreaks that the flames cannot jump."

Mrs. Grissinger and Mrs. Hansen helped their children

to roll out of their blankets and quilts. Mother busied herself with changing the baby, and Clara helped Father into his wheelchair. They gathered by the stove. Mother directed Clara to start frying yesterday's leftover porridge into fritters while she herself made the coffee.

Everyone was talking in hushed tones about the explosions, and fear spread quietly among the group. Miss Ottilie Wheeler sat on a kitchen chair under the oak tree and stared into space. Her sister, Amelia, rubbed her shoulders and spoke to her in comforting tones. But everyone was frightened; they feared that the Curfmans' home—their safe haven—might not be so safe after all. From all over the city came booming explosions as homes fell. Mother whispered to Clara and Father that their house would be next, she just *knew* it. Why *shouldn't* further calamity strike them after so many other terrible things had happened?

"We're going to be all right, Alice. Calm yourself." Father rolled his wheelchair over to the water barrel. "After all, people are being sent to Golden Gate Park for safety. You can see them passing in front of our house. And the park is only two blocks from us."

"You were the one just predicting the end of the world, Frederick! Which is it?" Mother pressed her lips together, but her eyes were wide with worry. She had looked like that, Clara remembered, the morning Father and Gideon set off for their steamship journey down the coast—the trip that had cost Gideon his life.

The men who had marched off with the officer the
night before had not returned. Their wives fed breakfast
to the children and sat by themselves, murmuring uneasily
to each other. Miss DuBois and Miss Chandler peeled
potatoes. Old Mr. Granger entertained the Wheeler sisters
with tales of battle in the War Between the States. Mother
fed Baby H more of the thinned porridge. The baby slurped
every bite off the spoon. Father guarded the water barrel
and doled out scant cupfuls when people were thirsty.

Clara scanned the backyard. It had become quite a
camp. Mattresses lay on the grass. Blankets aired on the
washing line. Chairs and tables and even the leather settee
had been carried from the house and set up in a makeshift
parlor under the oak tree. The children climbed the tree
and played on Clara's childhood swing. Baby H cried fret-
fully as Mother patted her back.

"Don't you cry, little lady," Mr. Granger said to the
baby. "I'll make you a swinging cradle out of that laundry
basket!"

Clara watched Mother try to soothe the baby. Surely
the baby was missing her own mother and father. Poor
little orphan! Mother jostled the baby on her shoulder
until Mr. Granger's swing was ready.

"There now, there's a lamb, my little Henrietta,"
crooned Mother, settling the baby into the basket.

"Henrietta?" asked Clara in surprise, giving the basket
a little push.

"Why, yes," said Mother. "I've decided to call her Henrietta, after my dear old aunt. You remember, Clara. The one who lived to the ripe old age of ninety-seven."

Clara only vaguely remembered Aunt Henrietta, but she nodded.

"It's a good family name," Mother continued, swinging the basket gently. "And of course we must call her something that begins with H, seeing as that's the letter on the rattle."

"Of course," agreed Clara. But the rattle in her skirt pocket felt heavy as she gazed out toward the street, wishing she could follow the people headed for the park two blocks away. Someone, somewhere, she felt certain, knew who this baby really was.

Satchel to Cliff House. The words echoed in her head as she fingered the scrap of paper in her pocket.

The morning passed with background noises of explosions, alarms, and shouting—and the billowing smoke made everyone's eyes sting. *But we are the lucky ones,* Clara kept telling herself as she folded the bedclothes and tidied the yard. *We're not in the path of the explosions,* she reminded herself as she started boiling beans for lunch in a pot on their makeshift stove. Water might be scarce, but at least there would be enough to eat for a while. *And at least we can stay on our own property,* she thought as she stood by Father's wheelchair in front of the house and watched streams of homeless people straggle toward Golden Gate

Park. At least she and her family would not need to join the soup lines ... at least not yet.

"Let's follow along, Clara," Father said suddenly. He craned his neck to watch the crowds round the corner at the end of the block, heading for the park. "I want to see what's happening. Can't just sit home forever twiddling our thumbs!"

Clara smiled tiredly. She knew Father hated feeling useless. He hated the numbness that afflicted his legs and made them too shaky for walking. *Nerve damage,* the doctors had pronounced after the shipwreck. Both legs had been broken when the wreckage slammed against them as Father tried to reach his son. After the broken bones had healed, doctors hoped that the feeling would return and the legs grow strong again. But here it was, nearly two years later, and still Father sat in his chair.

"I'd better check—" Clara began, then broke off, biting her lower lip. Mother would surely object to a trip to the park, or anywhere. *Stay home,* she would say. *Help out here, where I can keep you safe.* Clara shook back her tangled red hair and took hold of the wheelchair handles. "Aye-aye, Captain," she said firmly.

It wasn't easy pushing the wheelchair through the streets. Her quick run over to Emmeline's house yesterday had taken her through quiet streets to the north. Now they were walking south, and the streets were choked with people pulling their belongings behind them in wagons or pushing them in prams. And if wagons and prams could make it to the park, Clara told herself determinedly, then so could a wheelchair. She steered the chair around piles of rubble. She had to stop and lay boards across a wide fissure that split the road, creating a bridge for the wheelchair to ride across. She hesitated, looking down into the crack. It was eighteen inches wide, and when she peered down into it, she saw nothing—only blackness.

The fine hairs on the back of her neck prickled the way they had before she first leaped from the highest diving board at the Sutro Baths. The way they did each time she paused at her brother's closed bedroom door and put her hand on the doorknob. She shivered when faced with the unknown. This crack in the street led down— how far? And—to what?

The center of the earth?

She gripped the handles hard, pushing down the flutter of panic, and trundled the wheelchair across the bridge. She did not look back.

Two blocks from their house, Clara and Father came to Golden Gate Park. The park had always been a haven from the bustle of city life. It was a glorious expanse of hundreds of acres stretching west to Ocean Beach and the vast Pacific. Clara had learned at school how the parkland had once been sand dunes—but that was hard to imagine whenever she strolled the exquisitely landscaped gravel paths winding around Stowe Lake, watching young men courting their lady friends out in the rowboats. She loved the tulip gardens surrounding the Dutch windmill. She loved the woods full of eucalyptus, Monterey pines, and cypress trees. She and Gideon had ridden on the merry-go-round and the live donkeys while their parents sipped tea in the Japanese Tea Garden on Sunday afternoons. Even after Gideon's death, Clara escaped to the park whenever she could. It was a place of both tame and wild beauty—with birds singing in every tree, and buffalo in their enclosed meadows grazing nearby. A peaceful place.

But not anymore. Clara and Father stopped on the corner across from the park entrance and stared.

The park was swarming with distraught families. Thousands of homeless people thronged the gates, arriving from all directions and stamping through flower beds as they headed for the food lines or the tents being erected by soldiers. Everyone was hauling belongings in carts, wagons, or wheelbarrows. Baby prams were piled high with dishes, pictures, birdcages, washtubs, dolls and toy trains, clothing, and books. Clara watched in amazement as several steamer trunks with roller skates attached to each corner were wheeled past her. She and Father almost laughed at the sight of another family all straining together to push their upright piano across the street and into the park. But it was too sad a sight, really, for laughter. This was the stuff of people's lives, and they were lucky to have any of it left.

Clara maneuvered Father's chair across the street and

followed the crowds into the park. Large planks of wood had been nailed up between trees just inside the park's entrance gates to form a makeshift signboard. Near the signboard was a barrel of blank paper and a box of stubby pencils. Hundreds of notes already had been tacked up on the boards. Clara put the brake on Father's chair and stepped up to the signboard to get a closer look.

LOST!
Paul E. Hoffes, nine years old. Light complexioned, blue eyes. Please notify his mother. Panhandle in park, opposite Lyon Street entrance.

Mother is Looking:
Estelle, come to your Mother on the main drive of the Park.

Dan McIntyre: *Your family is looking for you! At the South Dune, back of the Children's Playground, you will find a board reading "McIntyre and Olsen Camp."*

—Your sister May

Clara tried to push Father's chair along the path but was hindered by the stream of people. Ahead of her she could see the green meadows covered by campsites. Families had erected shacks and strung blankets between the trees for privacy. No campfires were allowed, Clara read on signs posted on the trees. All food had to be eaten cold or be obtained from one of the soup lines.

"Mommy, Mommy, where are you?" howled a child, stumbling past and disappearing into the crowd.

"Turn back, Clara," said Father. "This is a madhouse." His voice was low-pitched, wretched with helplessness.

Clara obediently turned Father's wheelchair around. "I wish we could do something to help," she said, staring over her shoulder after the child.

"Well, we can't," he muttered. "Mother is right. There is enough to be tended to at home."

They retraced their path through the desolate streets, over the boards bridging the fissure, past the piles of rubble, back toward their own house. As they approached, they saw Mother struggling on the front steps with another woman. Mother's voice was raised in anger. "Take your hands off this baby!" she shouted at the younger woman, who seemed to be trying to wrest the infant from Mother's arms. "I told you no, and I mean no!"

"Hold on, Father," Clara said, and tightened her grip on the handles of his chair. She started running as fast as she dared, calling out, "We're coming, Mother! Hold on!"

"What in tarnation is going on here?" demanded Father as he and Clara jolted to a stop by the front porch.

Clara set the brake and raced up the steps to her mother's side. "Get away," she yelled at the young woman who was tugging at the baby's blanket. "What do you think you're doing?"

The baby was crying, and suddenly the woman started crying, too. She looked to be not much older than Clara herself, actually—more a girl than a grown woman. She wore a ragged red dress, torn at one shoulder, the skirt partially covered by a grimy white apron. Her hair and eyes were both pale, nearly colorless, and her face was smudged. The tears cut paths through the soot on her cheeks.

"This is *my* baby," she wailed. "You must give her to me!"

Clara reached out and intercepted the howling baby. Holding her close, she backed down the steps. "If this is your baby, why did you leave her with us?"

"It was the earthquake!" cried the young woman. "I was fleeing through the streets, and I was so frightened. I panicked … I thought this looked like a safe place … so I put her in your basket …"

"That *is* where you found her," Father reminded Clara.

But Clara was not convinced. This young woman's pallid skin, with smudges like bruises across the pale cheeks, bore no resemblance to the baby's pink-cheeked complexion. The woman's close-set eyes were watery blue—nothing like the infant's wide, dark gaze. And besides, the baby was an orphan—wasn't she?

"There was the note," Clara said slowly, tightening her

grip on Baby H. "Why would you say the baby was an orphan if you were very much alive?" Clara shook her head. "You don't look a thing like her. And why would you dress your baby in boys' clothes and shave her head? It just doesn't make sense." She took Mother's arm and turned toward the backyard. "So until you can prove to us who you are—forget it."

The young woman in red flew after them, her voice rising in panic. "Oh, please! I must take her back or else— Oh, Lord, there will be terrible trouble! I mean—there's danger—Oh! You *must* give her to me!"

"Take her back where?" demanded Mother.

"Trouble from whom?" asked Father, wheeling his chair across the path.

"To her home! To her parents—" shrieked the hysterical woman. Then she covered her face with her hands and crouched low, wracked with sobs.

"So you're *not* the mother," Clara declared. "I knew it."

"I never said I was! *You* said it!" sobbed the woman. "I'm her nanny! Her nursemaid! And I need to get her home safely now—over to Oakland. There's very grave danger—you don't understand—"

They all started at a great boom in the distance as another house was destroyed by explosives.

"We're all in grave danger, that I do understand," said Father. "But I must ask you to leave now. I don't think the ferries are running to Oakland—we've heard that the fire has consumed the wharf area. If you have no place to stay, you will find help at the park."

"But the baby—" She reached out her arms toward Clara.

"Surely you can't think I'm going to believe you're my little Henrietta's nursemaid any more than I believe you're her mother?" Mother said coldly. "Now leave us immediately, as my husband asked you to. Or we shall summon the authorities!"

"The police?" The girl grew even paler. She backed away, but her eyes were blazing with anger and—Clara thought—fear. "All right, I'm going," she shouted, walking out to the street. "But you'd better keep Helen safe for me! You keep her safe until I can come back for her, or you'll be sorry!" She ran down the street toward the park, her skirts a flash of red in the gray, smoky air.

Clara stared after her. Her heart was thumping hard.

"Helen?" asked Mother. "Did she say 'Helen'?"

"She did," replied Father.

Clara looked down at the baby's face. The tiny girl was quiet now, staring up at Clara with dark, puzzled eyes.

CHAPTER 6
NOISES IN THE NIGHT

"Helen starts with H," murmured Clara.

"So do Hester and Hannah and Hope ... and Hepzibah!" Mother frowned at Clara. "It doesn't mean anything. I thank you, Clara, for helping to get rid of that pushy girl, but don't start thinking her story makes sense. She admitted she lied about being Henrietta's mother, and she's lying about being her nursemaid, mark my words. Henrietta is staying with us. I'm not letting her out of my sight for one single second." Mother took the baby from Clara and marched up the steps to the front door. "Now there's work to do." She went into the house and shut the door firmly.

"Father? What do you think?" Clara felt uneasy. The young woman had seemed so afraid. Not just scared of the earthquake and fire, but scared of something else. Something worse.

Something still to happen?

Father shook his head and spread his hands. "Mother knows best," he said quietly, and Clara sighed. That had been Father's refrain ever since the accident. Mother hadn't wanted Gideon going on the steamship run; she thought he was too young for such hard work. Father had only laughed and said she babied him. Gideon was big, strong, and very nearly a man—and he wanted to go with Father. So they had gone off together on that last, disastrous voyage. Mother never said "I told you so," but the accusation was in every glance at Father, in every movement.

Clara pushed Father's wheelchair into the backyard, thinking about the woman in the red dress. Who was she really—nanny, or something else? Had she left the baby on the doorstep—or had someone else? And why?

Clara left Father sitting with the lady lodgers and their children and went indoors after Mother. She spent the rest of the day beating plaster dust from rugs, making up beds with fresh linens, and sweeping broken crockery into trash bins. She arranged books onto shelves and repotted tumbled houseplants. And as she worked, the puzzle of Baby H receded. Instead, memories of Gideon played behind her eyes like pictures on a stereoscope: The two of them sitting here in the front parlor, doing their school-work at the table by the fireplace. The two of them running upstairs and sliding down the banister. The two of them riding the tram to Ocean Beach at Lands End. The two of them swimming at the Sutro Baths, that incredible crystal palace where pools were filled by the tides and swimmers slid down slides or dropped from trapezes or leapt from springboards into the water. She remembered the two of them poised on the high dive, listening to voices below shouting up to them—"The girl is too young! Bring her safely down the ladder at once!"—before Clara launched into her perfect swan dive, followed by Gideon, slicing through the cold deep water. Gideon had taught her well.

While Baby H napped in her wooden drawer, the lodgers ventured indoors to ask Mother whether they might risk sleeping in the house tonight. Mother said that only a few rooms had been cleaned, but unless another quake brought the house down on top of them, she did not mind who slept where.

Despite the dust still hanging in the air and the grit underfoot, Clara was glad to crawl into bed that night and lie between clean sheets. Sleeping on a soft mattress on the floor of her parents' room beat sleeping in a dusty bedroll outdoors on the grass, poked by roots. Baby H snoozed at Clara's side, tucked into the drawer. The lodgers, including Mrs. Grissinger and Mrs. Hansen and their children, bedded down throughout the house wherever they found a clean spot to lay their blankets.

Clara listened to the creaks and groans of the house

and to the shouts in the distance. She pictured the people in the park, settling down in their tents. She wondered where Emmeline and her family were and hoped they were safe. She saw in her mind the dirty, haggard face of the young woman in the red dress, and she turned over and placed one hand protectively on the bundle of baby sleeping at her side. Finally, Clara slept too.

She dived off the rocks like a sleek gray seal, rippling through deep water toward the dark figure struggling beneath the surface—

Humphrey's low growl in her ear made her jump awake. "Wh-what is it, boy?" she whispered into the darkness. Had it been minutes or hours since she drifted off? Was there going to be another earthquake each time she had one of the swimming dreams? She looked around. In the dim room she could just make out the shapes of her sleeping parents and Baby H. She patted the floor next to her. "Lie down, Humph. Good boy." She closed her eyes again, throwing her arm across Humphrey's broad back. The dog growled again, low in his throat.

Then it was only a second before she and the dog were both on their feet, listening at the closed door of the bedroom. There *was* something—some strange noise.

"Shh," Clara shushed Humphrey. "Listen—"

Was one of the lodgers walking about in the parlor? But no one was sleeping in there. Clara gripped Humphrey's collar. Her parents slumbered on. Should she wake them? But Mother would panic and Father would be helpless and

angry. Maybe she could alert Mr. Midgard and Mr. Stokes—
but no! They weren't home ... It was up to her to see what
was wrong.

Clara started to tiptoe out the door with Humphrey
right beside her, her fingers tight around his collar, but
then she stopped, looking back into the bedroom. Her eyes
fastened on the fireplace poker by the hearth.

Better than nothing.

A scraping noise. A thump. Definitely coming from
the parlor.

Heart thudding, Clara gripped the iron poker and
headed down the hallway, Humphrey at her side. She waited
in the hallway just inches from the open parlor door. Two
more steps and she would be able to peek inside.

Craning her neck, she looked into the room. In the
moonlight she could see the bookshelves, the potted
aspidistra, the high-backed settee. But no one was there.
She relaxed for a moment and loosened her hold on the
dog's collar. Then her gaze swept toward the broken
window, and she sucked in her breath.

There was an arm stretching itself in through a broken
windowpane—an arm in a black sleeve groping for the
window catch.

Clara froze. *It must be a looter!* she thought, and then
raced forward into the room and slammed her iron poker
down onto the arm. An agonized howl from the figure
outside, Humphrey's frenzied barking, and Clara's shouts

for help merged into a terrible ruckus that brought Mother
and the lodgers racing into the parlor.

"Mother! Help!" shouted Clara. "Don't let him get
away!"

"Stay back, Clara!" Mother spun Clara away from the
window—but Clara saw that the man was already out in
the street, clutching his arm and running fast. Then a
second figure emerged from around the side of the house
and scrambled after him, long skirt flapping.

"Two of them!" Clara exclaimed.

"Is anyone hurt?" Miss DuBois and Miss Chandler
crept nervously into the room. Mrs. Grissinger and
Mrs. Hansen followed. Mr. Granger and the Wheeler
sisters peered into the room from the doorway.

"There was somebody outside—" began Clara, but
Mother cut her off.

"Looters now on top of everything else—and you
chasing them!" Her voice broke. "Oh, Clara, I couldn't
bear for anything to happen to you."

"Goodness, I do wish the menfolk were here," said
Miss DuBois, putting an arm around Mother's shoulders.

"I'm here," protested Mr. Granger in his quavery voice.

"And *I'm* here." Father rolled into the room in his
wheelchair. He took in the sight of Clara standing with
the poker and shook his head. "But you seem to have
things well in hand, daughter."

"A man was at the window!" Clara explained what

had happened. "His arm—oh, Father!" She shuddered, remembering. "I didn't even think—I just slammed the poker down. Then two people ran off—"

"*Two* men? In which direction did they go?" asked Father quickly.

"Toward the park, I think," said Clara. "But it was a man and a woman, Father. The woman came running around the side of the house. Perhaps she'd been hiding there!"

"I was awakened by a noise at the dining room window," said Miss Chandler. "She may have been trying to climb inside."

"Lady looters." Father shook his head morosely. "Nothing will surprise me anymore."

The baby's thin wail reached their ears.

Mother hurried into the hallway. "Poor little mite—wakes up and no one is there ... I'm coming, Henrietta!" She called back over her shoulder to Clara, "You come along now back to sleep. I want you with me!"

"Baby H . . ." murmured Clara. A prickle of unease stirred across her mind like the breeze through the broken windows.

She turned to Father. "I want to check the backyard."

"The rain barrels!" said Father with a frown. "No, dear, it could be dangerous. I shall go myself."

Clara and Miss DuBois looked at each other dubiously.

Father rubbed his hands tiredly over his face. "I daresay

by the time I've clattered down the ramp in my chair, the whole neighborhood will have heard me, and anyone siphoning our water or hiding in the bushes will have had time to flee. Well, that's what we want, isn't it? To make them run off?"

"We'll go together," Clara suggested gently. "I'll bring the poker."

Father sighed and snapped his fingers for Humphrey. "We'll take the dog."

"Well, you're a brave pair, I'll say that for you," said Miss DuBois.

Clara pushed Father's wheelchair down the hallway. As they passed the back bedroom, Mother opened the door, the baby in her arms. She stared out at them, aghast. "I want you safely in bed, Clara!" she hissed.

"Yes, ma'am," Clara whispered back. "In just a minute."

"The rain barrels," explained Father.

They opened the back door, despite Mother's objections, and stood staring out into the backyard. The basket Mr. Granger had hung from the oak tree swung gently in the smoky breeze, illuminated by moonlight. The rain barrels appeared to be untouched.

"You stay here, Father. I'll be just a second." Clara handed him the poker and darted down the steps. She didn't really think there were any more looters hiding around the side of the house; in fact, she had a sneaking suspicion that the two people trying to break into the house had not been looters at all. The prickle of worry she had felt just minutes before grew stronger as she rounded the corner of the house and walked along the narrow passageway that separated their house from the one next door.

"Clara!" She heard Father's voice in the darkness but did not turn back. She passed the kitchen window. And then there was the dining room window, where Miss Chandler had heard a noise.

And there—*there!*—on a rosebush just below the window was a piece of torn fabric, caught on the thorns. Clara lifted it off carefully. In the moonlight the color was hard to make out, but Clara felt certain she knew what the light would reveal:

A soft scrap of red.

CHAPTER 7
TENT TOWN TURMOIL

I t was hard to sleep after that. Clara dozed fitfully, but at every sound her eyes flew open. When pale dawn light filtered in through the broken windows, Clara rolled off her mattress and stood up. Baby H slumbered in the drawer, unaware of the mystery surrounding her. Clara glanced at her sleeping parents, then dressed swiftly, slipping silently through the house. She grabbed her shawl off the peg by the back door, then headed outside and down the ramp. She wanted to be gone before Mother and Father woke up.

Clara thrust her hand into her skirt pocket as she rounded the side of the house. She felt the soft red scrap of cloth, the cold silver rattle, and the slip of paper with *SATCHEL TO CLIFF HOUSE* pasted onto it. Each of these things was innocuous enough, alone. But together they were pieces of a puzzle that filled Clara with a growing unease. And last night's intruders were another part of the puzzle.

It didn't make sense that they were looters. Why would looters come to a house full of people when there were thousands of abandoned homes all over San Francisco now? No, Clara decided as she set off down the street, the intruders last night had come for some other reason. They wanted something else besides Mother's silver platter or her jewel box.

They wanted the baby.

Clara shivered in the morning fog as she headed toward Golden Gate Park. It felt strange going there without her big brother—or even Father—at her side.

The air hung thick and cold. Fog lay heavier than usual this morning, mixed with the smoke. It covered the bay and stretched up into the hills. Clara clutched her shawl more tightly.

She entered the gates of the park and moved forward as part of the jostling crowd already in line for breakfast. The woman in red had wanted to take the baby. She had run off in the direction of Golden Gate Park. One of the nighttime intruders had been a woman. She had left behind a torn piece of red fabric on a rosebush. *Where is that woman now?* wondered Clara, rising up on tiptoes to scan the park.

The place seemed to have grown overnight. Soldiers from the nearby Presidio army base had set up more relief stations to serve food and dispense first aid. There were real tents now among the makeshift shelters of tablecloths and clotheslines—stout canvas army tents that could house several families at once.

"This way to the grub, folks!" bellowed a voice out of the fog. "Line up in an orderly manner! Bring your own bowls if you have them! This way to breakfast!"

The crowd shifted as people moved toward the food line. Clara turned in the opposite direction, toward the notice boards with their hundreds of messages. If someone had lost a baby girl, that would be the place to post a note—

"I'm not going for breakfast, either," said a shrill voice at her side. "Not when there's sweets instead!"

Her thoughts interrupted, Clara looked over at a boy holding out his hand to her. He was offering her something in his cupped palm. "Hey, want some jujubes? I've got thousands!"

"Thousands?" she repeated, looking past him at the signboard. There were thousands of messages, it looked like. All of them sad.

"Jujubes," he said again. "*Candy*."

She frowned at him. He was a raggedy kid about her own age, wearing old clothes and a dirty cap. He was pulling a child's wagon stuffed with a battered brown suitcase, a pile of books, and several crates.

"I know what jujubes are," Clara told him. They had

been Gideon's favorite. She preferred jelly beans herself. "But—no thanks. Not now." She headed toward the basket of scrap paper, pencils, and crayons.

"I've got boxes of jujubes," confided the boy, edging closer to her. "Got 'em from Blum's Candy Store—you know it? Over on the corner of Polk and Sutter? Before they blew it up for the firebreak, this cop said, 'Go ahead, boys, help yourselves, but be quick!' Can you believe it?" His eyes were wide as he told his story. His words tumbled out in a frantic jumble. "Some fellows were loading a whole cable car–caboose full of gumdrops and all-day suckers! I just got a coupla boxes of jujubes and chocolate drops. But better than nothing, hey?"

"Sure," said Clara, looking more closely at him. The wide eyes weren't due just to amazement over getting so much free candy, she realized now. And the rapid-fire words weren't just the result of excitement. She recognized the symptoms from the time right after the shipwreck when she'd heard the news about Gideon—and couldn't stop talking. *Shock,* the doctor had diagnosed.

This boy was in shock. He was wearing only a thin shirt and knee pants, and he was shivering badly. "Here," Clara said suddenly, pulling off her shawl and handing it to him. "Wrap this around you. You're shaking like a—"

"Like an earthquake?" giggled the boy. He shook his head. "I can't take your shawl."

"Just till you warm up," Clara urged him, putting it

around his shoulders. "And let's get you some real food. Save the candy for dessert."

He allowed her to tow him toward the food line. They stood there, two out of two thousand, all waiting for breakfast.

Despite the crowds, the park was hushed. People seemed dazed. Some looked heavy-eyed from not having slept at all. They gratefully received bowls of oatmeal and slices of bread. The boy wolfed down his portion in seconds. Clara accepted a bowl from a young soldier, although she was not hungry. She and the boy walked over to a stand of cypress trees and sat down on the grass. She gave him her bowl and the bread; she knew there would be food waiting for her when she returned home.

The boy devoured the second bowl nearly as fast as the first. Then, warmed by Clara's shawl and the hot oatmeal, he lay back in the grass with a sigh. "That *is* better," he said. "Thank you very much." He sat up again and held out his dirty hand. "My name is Edgar Green."

"I'm Clara Curfman," she responded, shaking his hand. "Are you with your family?"

He lay back again and closed his eyes briefly. "Nope," he said softly. "I've got no family, not anymore. Earthquake took care of that. Bedroom ceiling came down right on top of Uncle James. Killed him without even waking him up. I tried to dig him out, but it took four men from next door. He was stone cold."

"Oh! I'm so sorry!" Clara didn't know what else to say.

"Well, I guess maybe it's a blessing, dying quick like that—if you've got to go anyway..." Edgar's voice drifted off and he stared into the distance. "Uncle James was my guardian. My parents died of influenza last winter. So now I guess I'm more of an orphan than ever."

"I'm really so very sorry," Clara repeated helplessly.

"I keep thinking I see Uncle James," Edgar confided in a low voice. "I keep feeling he's right behind me. In fact—I have that feeling now. That he's watching over me—over *us*. Right now."

Clara often had felt the same about Gideon, and it had comforted her. But she glanced uneasily over her shoulder now. Were unseen eyes watching from the bushes? Whose eyes?

"What will you do now?" she asked the boy hurriedly. "Are you living here in the park?"

"I've only just arrived. The people next door were going to take me with them after our houses collapsed... but I heard them talking about finding me a place in an orphanage somewhere, so I ran off. I'm not going to no orphanage, no matter what!" He stood up. "Which tent is your family tucked up in?"

"Oh, they're at home." She saw his look of surprise and explained further. "Our house is still standing. It's just—I'm here trying to find somebody."

"Who?" He sounded interested and, Clara noticed,

looked much better now after eating. His face had more color, and he wasn't shaking anymore.

She threaded her way through the crowd to return their thick crockery bowls to the soup kitchen. One of the Chinese men working there thanked her with a stately bow so low that his long pigtail swung down to the ground. Then he dunked their bowls into a tub of murky dishwater. Clara headed back to the signboards with Edgar at her heels.

"Who have you lost?" he asked again, handing back Clara's shawl.

She picked a thick black crayon out of the basket and slid a piece of paper from the stack, replacing the rock that held the papers securely so they would not blow away. "Well, my friend Emmeline and her family seem to be missing," she said. "And then there was this baby left in a basket on our doorstep!"

"Poor thing, probably orphaned like me."

"Well, that's what we thought at first, but it's stranger than that." And Clara told him about the shaven head, the sailor suit, the silver rattle, and the message on the slip of paper.

"Cliff House!" Edgar looked intrigued. "My uncle is a chef there for the big restaurant—that is, he *was*. He took me with him sometimes." He stared down at the ground for a moment. "Anyway, what's Cliff House got to do with your baby, do you think?"

"I don't know," replied Clara. "The whole thing is very

strange." She scanned the people's faces as they stepped
up to write messages. "But someone must know who she
is. Someone must know where she really belongs."

There were so many missing people. Dozens of little
messages were tacked up on the boards.

Byron J. Maxim, if you are living, come home. . . .
Bring May, Bessie, and boys. Mother will shelter them.
                                   Mrs. Kate Maxim

Lost—Victor and Bernard Hickman, age 10 and 7 years;
dark gray suits, blue corduroy hats. Return North Beach
Powerhouse. —Mr. Whaley

Susie and Charlie O'Day! Janey is safe. Come to our
tent next to Stowe Lake and we'll all be together!
                                   Grandma Perkins

Clara hunched over and used one of the big crates of
jujubes in Edgar's wagon as her desk while she carefully
printed her own message:

PARENTS of BABY H—*Approx. 6-month-old girl*
found safe and sound. Please post a message here telling
where to find you.

"Why not just write down your address and have them

come collect the baby?" asked Edgar. "Wouldn't that be easier?"

"I don't want anyone else trying to take her," said Clara grimly. Then, in a low voice, she told Edgar about the woman who had come to the house, and the looters last night who had not really been looters.

"You think she's here, then, the woman in red?" Edgar asked when she'd finished. "Here in the park?"

"I do." Clara tacked up her message. "There. I'd better be heading home because my mother gets in a state—" Clara broke off with a gasp as a poster attached to a large oak tree near the message board caught her eye.

"Edgar—look!"

"What?"

Clara pointed, then ran over to the poster. She read it with growing excitement.

LOST in the QUAKE!

Who has Seen our Baby Girl,
Helen Forrest, only 6 months old,
and her Nursemaid, Hattie Pitt, age 19 yrs???
Last seen boarding San Francisco–bound
Ferry in Oakland, Tuesday afternoon.
Please contact desperate Parents
Mr. and Mrs. Lucas Forrest
17 Claremont Ridge Road in Oakland
or leave message here.

"That's them! That must be Baby H's parents!" Clara felt a surge of joy. "The woman in red called the baby Helen. And she said she was her nanny. It all fits . . . except—"

"Except the baby was in disguise," Edgar finished. "And the note said she was an orphan."

"Oh, dear, those poor parents," said Clara. "They're over in Oakland and don't know where their baby is!"

"But if they're in Oakland, then who put up this fancy poster?" Edgar inquired.

Clara frowned. She reached out a finger and stroked the poster. Unlike the thin scraps of paper all the other notes were written upon, the poster on the tree was printed on heavy white cardboard. The lettering was bold and deliberate—not at all like the hasty scrawls on the other notes.

Clara hesitated a moment, rereading the poster, then unpinned it from the tree. "I don't know who put up the notice, but I'm quite sure this is our baby." She rolled the poster into a tight tube. "My parents need to see this."

Clara went back to the message board. She had one more message to write. She used the black crayon to print neatly on another slip of paper:

Emmeline and family, where are you?? Curfmans'
Boardinghouse has room for all! Please come to us!
Love, Clara

"Curfmans' Boardinghouse?" read Edgar over her shoulder. "Room for all?"

"We run a boardinghouse," said Clara. She hesitated. "I suppose you could come home with me, if you like. Seeing as you haven't anywhere else to go. We've got people in bedrolls all over the place now as it is."

"Yes, please, I'll come," said Edgar eagerly. "I don't have any money, but I could help out if your mother would find some chores for me—" He broke off and turned around swiftly. "There—I—oh, I have the feeling again! Of someone watching me. Uncle James—?"

Clara whirled around and glimpsed a flash of red disappearing into the crowd. The hairs on the back of her neck prickled. Then she gave herself a mental shake. Lots of people wore red. And now that she knew who the baby most probably was, there was no need to find the woman who had claimed to be the nursemaid. She would search for the parents themselves.

"Come on, then, Edgar," Clara said heartily. "Come with me and let Mother put you to work." She gave him a sudden grin. "Mother is extraordinarily good at finding chores for people to do. It's one of her particular talents."

They laughed together and the sound rang in Clara's ears as if it were a foreign language. It was the first laughter she'd heard in days.

And then, somehow, everything was funny. As the two

of them headed back to Clara's house, they giggled at the sight of the man coming toward them carrying two parrots, one on either shoulder, and pushing a third in a cage in a wheelbarrow. They tossed clods of dirt into the fissure splitting the street and shouted, "Helloooo down there!" They made jokes about the fog, the rubble, even the deafening explosion a few blocks away that shook the ground as yet another home fell to make the firebreak. The smoke in the distance was hilarious, and they ran, shrieking, for half a block without stopping, Edgar's wagon jolting along behind them. It felt so good to laugh.

They stopped only when Edgar's crates and brown suitcase bounced off and thudded across the ground. His suitcase popped open, spilling clothing and books into the road, and a large photograph in a glass frame cracked on the rubble. "Oh, no," Edgar said, and there wasn't a trace of laughter in his voice anymore. He picked up the photograph, and Clara saw that the photo was of an elderly man with a quiet smile. "Uncle James," Edgar murmured, and ducked his head.

He stood quietly, and Clara wondered uncomfortably if he might be praying for his uncle. She felt guilty about their silliness. How could they act as if tragedy hadn't happened—as if tragedies weren't still happening all around them?

Clara squeezed the rolled-up poster tightly in one hand while she watched Edgar trying to compose himself.

She stuck her other hand into her pocket and closed her fingers around the silver rattle. She felt the little crumpled piece of paper—the mysterious message—and smoothed it against her palm.

We'll have you home soon, Baby Helen! she vowed to herself.

She turned back and helped Edgar repack his belongings into the wagon. Then the two of them set off again, side by side, and neither of them felt like laughing anymore.

Back at the boardinghouse, no one was laughing either.

CHAPTER 8

A MYSTERIOUS MESSAGE

The house was in an uproar. At first Clara feared it was because Mother had discovered she was missing. But as she and Edgar entered the house, they realized the hubbub was centered in the parlor. The men who had marched away with the soldiers had returned.

And they had brought bad news. Clara and Edgar sidled into the room and stood by the broken windows to listen. Hiram Stokes, Geoffrey Midgard, Mr. Grissinger, and Mr. Hansen stood in the center of the room describing all they had seen and done while fighting the fires. Father sat in his wheelchair with Mother standing at his side, Baby Helen snug in her arms. Old Mr. Granger had his arms around the Wheeler sisters' shoulders. Miss DuBois seemed to have been sobbing, Clara noted with a sinking heart. Miss Chandler, pale and wide-eyed, stood alone in the corner by the grandfather clock. Mrs. Grissinger and

Mrs. Hansen sat together, faces ashen. Only their children seemed happy, excited to have their fathers back.

"The blasting sounds like artillery fire," Mr. Grissinger was saying, shaking his head.

"It's a war out there," agreed Geoffrey Midgard, "and one we're not winning. The firebreak idea was good, but it just isn't working."

"Oh, I think the fires may be out by the end of the day," Hiram Stokes responded heartily, glancing at Miss DuBois. But Clara could tell he was just trying to comfort her, not sure at all that he spoke the truth.

"You're an optimist," muttered Mr. Hansen. "The fires are raging, and nothing is stopping them!"

The soldiers had taken the men to join forces with all the others working to clear the streets of rubble. Pathways had to be cleared for the fire wagons. But water mains were broken, so there was no water to put out the fires, and the firebreaks weren't working. Flames progressed along city streets block by block, devouring everything in their path.

"I saw people waiting on their front steps till the fire was nearly upon them before they'd move," marveled Mr. Grissinger. "Only then would they leave their homes and head for shelter."

"The soldiers wouldn't let people stay anywhere near their homes where I was working," reported Hiram Stokes. "They herded people out of their neighborhoods like cattle—trying to get them away before the houses were dynamited. Oh, Lordy, people were wailing and cussing at those soldiers something fierce!"

"Didn't matter in the end, though, all the dynamiting," Geoffrey Midgard added. "Because the fire just swept through the neighborhoods anyway and reduced to ashes everything that wasn't already exploded."

"Awful," said Father. "Think how many homes might have been saved if the soldiers hadn't ordered people to leave! Folks might have been able to wet down their roofs, keep the sparks off—"

"In some places the fire was a mile high, a huge wall of fire coming right down the street! You couldn't have saved a house by pouring water on the roof—and there is no water anyway!" Mr. Hansen's voice was choked. "You didn't see it, Mr. Curfman, or you'd know it was hopeless! People were running everywhere, trying to get their families and animals to safety..."

Father muttered under his breath.

"Horses screaming," continued Mr. Hansen, shaking his head. "I saw some of them—trapped under debris. Legs broken. Backs crushed. Had to be shot."

Miss DuBois broke into fresh sobs.

"I hear the waterfront's been saved, though," Geoffrey Midgard said hastily. "I was down that way last night, and they were spraying water from the bay. Fire boats came over from Oakland and up from San Jose. The whole East Side's gone, though."

The men kept talking all at once, interrupting each other, their words overlapping, their voices mingling in a desperate attempt to convey the horrors they'd seen. They described weeping women, wailing children, men with broken limbs lying in the street. They described acts of heroism: The little girl who rushed back inside after her cat only to discover that the housemaid lay trapped in the kitchen. She had been able to save both of them. A woman who gave birth, assisted by neighbors, as the fire approached. She and her baby were whisked to safety moments after the newborn's first breath. A man who was suddenly strong enough to lift a toppled piano single-handedly off his son's legs and drag the boy out of the path of fire.

Mr. Hansen grew very quiet. He kept his head down, his arm about his wife's waist. *He's seen terrible things,* thought Clara. *Too terrible to talk about.*

"It's like a scene from hell down in Chinatown," Mr. Grissinger said. "From hell, I tell you! Those poor folks have nothing left at all!"

Geoffrey Midgard's voice rose above his. "I heard there were a hundred thousand people homeless the first day after the quake, and who knows how high the toll is now!"

"Who knows how high it will go!" cried Mr. Granger in his shrill voice. "We're all doomed!"

"No, no, man," said Hiram Stokes, going over to the

old man and clapping him on the back. "No, I think we'll be safe on this side of the city. That's why they let us come home."

Across the room, Father in his wheelchair beckoned to Clara.

"Where have you been, child?" he demanded when she joined him. "Your mother looked everywhere. We were very worried."

"We most certainly were!" Mother said in a tight, angry tone. "I was about to come searching for you, but then all the men arrived back and it's been bedlam since."

"I'm sorry, Mother," Clara began. "I just went to the park—I posted a message for Emmeline's family, telling them to come to us. And while I was there, I saw this poster—here, look." Clara unrolled the poster and handed it to Mother.

Mother read it swiftly, shaking her head. "It's not the same baby, I'm sure it isn't. The note in the basket said this child is an orphan."

"But surely we should check, Mother!" objected Clara. "Father, certainly you'll agree we can't just keep this baby without contacting the Forrests."

Mother's voice trembled. "I think the baby's true family perished in the quake, and anyone else trying to claim her will have to convince me they can give her a better home than we can." She gripped Clara's shoulder with a heavy hand. "And you aren't to leave this house by yourself again, young lady, do I make myself clear? No going back to the park, and certainly not over to Oakland in search of these...Forrests. You're to stay right here with me. There are all sorts of dangers now—haven't you been listening?"

Clara couldn't believe Mother was being so uncooperative about searching for the baby's true family. It was all very well for Mother to want to adopt a child to replace Gideon, but if that child had been kidnapped...then Mother had no right! Clara looked at Father, sitting there so silently. Once he would have put his foot down. He'd been master of the house and head of the family, and his word was law. Now he wouldn't even *try* to take charge!

Father patted Clara's shoulder gently, but he did not say anything, except to Edgar. "Now who are you?"

"Edgar Green, sir," said Edgar, sticking out his hand to shake Father's, then Mother's.

"Edgar's uncle has been killed, and now he has no family," Clara told them. "I thought he could stay with us awhile. I'm sure, Mother, you can find some chores for him." Maybe Mother should adopt *Edgar,* Clara thought mutinously, ignoring the sharp look Mother gave her. At least he could tell them who he really was and what had happened to him!

"Of course, lad," said Father. "You'll be able to earn your keep, I daresay."

"Oh, I'm a very hard worker," Edgar assured him.

Suddenly Mr. Hansen broke his silence. "My parents will be frantic!" he cried to his wife. "I can't bear to think of my poor mother worrying—but how will we let our family back east know we're safe? We can't!"

"It's true the telephone lines are down, but at least the post office looks to be standing," said Hiram Stokes soothingly. "And I heard that you can send letters for free now to anywhere in the world to let relatives know you're safe. Just take the letter to the post office and it will be sent."

"Well, I heard it burnt down!" claimed Mr. Grissinger.

"Saw it myself," said Hiram Stokes, "just two hours ago. There are a lot of rumors flying around, and it's hard to know what to believe until you go out and check. Why, yesterday I heard people saying that Cliff House had fallen into the ocean during the quake—but today I heard it's still standing strong."

Cliff House, thought Clara. She glanced at the baby, cradled against Mother's shoulder.

Baby H opened her mouth like a little bird and waved her tiny fists. "Look at our hungry starling," Mother crooned. "I think we could all use some lunch, don't you?"

The Wheeler sisters and Mr. Granger headed out of the parlor with Mother. Miss DuBois and Miss Chandler followed. But the others were still discussing the calamity in rising voices. Clara and Edgar lingered to listen.

"The Nob Hill mansions are gone, all of them," Geoffrey

Midgard was insisting. "I was up there! The Hopkins Institute of Art—ashes now, too—but I saw people carrying out some of the paintings. So that's good."

"Russian Hill homes are gone, as well," pronounced Mr. Grissinger with some relish. "Seems the rich burn just as easily as the poor in the end. Pots of money won't save you from this fire, no sir!"

"Gentlemen," said Mother from the doorway, "we're all very glad indeed that you're home safe and sound. Now, please come to the dining room for your lunch. I'm afraid it's just potatoes, but there's a bit of leftover soup, too. Clara, I'll need your help. And you, young man—Edward, is it? Come along, lad."

"It's Edgar, ma'am. Just show me what to do."

As he and Clara stepped out the back door into the yard, Edgar whispered, "There—don't you sense it? We're being watched! I believe it *is* Uncle James. He's happy I'm here with you now..."

Clara glanced back over her shoulder. She, too, had the sensation of being under scrutiny.

"It's just a feeling I keep getting," continued Edgar in a whisper. "I felt it most strongly back in the parlor when I was standing by the windows—didn't you?"

Clara wiggled her shoulders uncomfortably as if to shake a ghost off her back. She stood at the makeshift stove and ladled buttered potatoes from the cooking pot into bowls for Edgar to carry inside to the lodgers.

Back and forth he went, two bowls at a time, until all were served. Clara filled the pitcher with water from the rain barrel and walked up the ramp behind him into the house.

"Let me get you a chair," said Mother when Edgar stepped into the dining room.

"I'll fetch it," said Hiram Stokes, and he hurried to bring one from the kitchen table. Edgar raised his eyebrows at Clara and looked pointedly to the empty place, Gideon's place, at the far end of the table. Clara shook her head.

Shrugging, Edgar sat in the chair Mr. Stokes brought. Then Mr. Stokes walked to the head of the table and handed Mother a sheet of paper. "Here, ma'am. This was lying on the floor inside the back door. I guess someone must have just dropped it off—though I looked outside and saw no one in the yard."

Clara looked up sharply from her potatoes.

Mother, bouncing Baby H on her knee, scanned the paper. Her face paled. "Oh dear," she said. "Clara, it seems you've had a hand in this!"

"What is it?" Clara reached across the table for the page. The handwriting was elegant, the message succinct. Alarm bells sounded in her head as she read.

Kind Friend,
We read the notice you posted in the park and are so glad you have our daughter safe and sound.

Please bring her to us at the Japanese Tea Garden at four o'clock today. We will be waiting. You will be amply rewarded for your care of our dear baby girl.
Signed—
Mr. and Mrs. Forrest

"Forrests again," Mother said softly, rubbing her cheek against Baby H's fuzzy head. "Your poster must be right, Clara, after all." She sighed heavily. "So, these Forrests will meet us in the park at the Japanese Tea Garden today at four. So soon—" She dipped her head to the baby. "Oh, little one, I do hate to give you up."

"But, of course, we must," said Father from his end of the table. "May I see the note, Clara?" Silently she passed it to him, her mind in a whirl. "One would think," added Father, "they could have knocked on the door and spoken to us instead of leaving a note!"

"That *is* rather odd," agreed Miss Chandler.

The lodgers buzzed with interest as the note was passed around the table. "I daresay," said Miss Amelia Wheeler, "that this note was brought by messenger."

"Perhaps the parents have been injured," added her sister, Ottilie.

"That would explain it," nodded Mrs. Hansen. "The poor people. At least we have all *our* children here with us. It would be dreadful to become separated!"

Mother had been sitting silently, her face buried in the

baby's neck. Now she raised her face, and Clara saw the tracks of tears on Mother's cheeks. "I know how dreadful it is to lose a child," she said softly. "Of course we will return this precious lamb at four o'clock, just as they've asked us to."

Father cleared his throat. "I will accompany you to the park, Alice."

Clara stared from one parent to the other, then pushed back her chair. "Hold it!" she exclaimed. "Wait—you mustn't take her to the park!"

"Now, Clara," said Father, "I admit, I was hesitant to turn her over to that strange young woman, but this note puts the situation in rather a different light. The least we can do is see who comes to meet us at the tea garden."

"It won't be the parents!" cried Clara. The alarm bells in her head were very loud now, and she felt a rising sense of danger that had nothing to do with the fires still raging in her city.

"What do you mean?" demanded Mother. "How can you know that?"

And Edgar added mildly, "I don't see what you're so upset about, Clara. After all, you posted that note just so the parents *would* find their baby! Now they have, so what's wrong?"

Clara stood trembling behind her chair. She gripped the back of it, hard. "What's wrong is that the note came here, right to our door. To our back door, Edgar, just after we felt someone was watching us out in the yard—"

"Uncle James," he murmured.

"I'm sorry, but I don't think so. I think someone was out there watching us. Then, when we came in, that person crept up the ramp and slid this note under the door." She took a deep breath to calm herself.

"All right, maybe so," Edgar said. "Maybe the messenger saw us going inside, so he slipped it under the door instead—"

"No," said Clara. "No. Because you're forgetting something, Edgar. When I wrote the note and posted it on the message board in the park, I deliberately did *not* write our address. Remember?"

Slowly, Edgar nodded.

The room was quiet. "So how," Clara asked softly, "did they know where to find the baby?"

CHAPTER 9
NOBODY'S BABY

I think we should go to the park at four o'clock," Clara announced into the uproar around the table. "Leaving the baby at home." She glanced at Father. "Under guard."

"And we'll see who shows up at the tea garden!" Edgar chimed in. "We'll talk to them and demand proof—"

"Perhaps a photograph of the baby and her parents together," Miss Ottilie Wheeler added. "Ooh, this is very exciting!"

"It could be dangerous," said Father, looking to Mother. "Though it's not a bad plan in itself."

Mother shook her head. "Clara is not to go to the park!"

"I'll go," said Hiram Stokes.

"And I," said Geoffrey Midgard. "We'll see who shows up and bring them back here if they can prove they are legitimate."

Clara scowled. She wanted desperately to be at the

Japanese Tea Garden at four o'clock. "Please, Mother, let me go with the men."

"Absolutely not," said Mother. "It would be madness. We don't know a thing about these people. I want you where I can keep an eye on you today."

And, true to her word, Mother kept Clara and Edgar busy for the rest of the afternoon. They cleaned the lunch dishes out in the yard, using as little water as possible. They checked through the dwindling supply of foodstuffs and fried up cornmeal fritters to serve for supper with the last of the bean soup. At three-thirty, Hiram Stokes and Geoffrey Midgard set off for Golden Gate Park.

Clara and Edgar stayed behind. They cut up apples, bruised from rolling out of their barrel in the quake, and made a thick applesauce seasoned with cinnamon and a little sugar. It would have been fun for Clara, having someone to share the work with—almost like spending the afternoon with Gideon—if she had not been so upset about what might be happening in the park without her. Mother sat inside with the lady lodgers, passing the baby around and playing with her. Old Mr. Granger obligingly pushed the Hansen and Grissinger tots in the swing hanging from the oak tree. It was a cheerful scene in the backyard despite the smoke pall hanging in the air, but Clara couldn't relax. She felt edgy. Edgar only made matters worse. Sure that his Uncle James's ghost was hovering, he kept turning around suddenly as if to catch it unawares.

Clara set the applesauce to simmer on the makeshift stove. "You're making me jittery," she complained to Edgar as the two of them began refilling the kerosene lanterns and trimming the wicks.

Mother called to Clara from the back door. "The baby has soiled her diaper and the doll dress, and now she's got nothing clean to wear, poor lamb. Please pop up to the attic for our storage carton of baby garments, while I warm some water. She needs a bath."

Clara obligingly hurried into the house and up the stairs. The attic was dim and cool. Evidence of the quake was less obvious here. Stacked boxes had tumbled onto the floor, and the heavy steamer trunks had slid from one end of the narrow, low-ceilinged room to the other, but damage was minimal. Clara restacked boxes, reading the labels of their contents as she worked, and soon she had located "Baby Garments."

She headed for the staircase with the carton. But then she stopped at the little diamond-shaped window that lit the attic with weak afternoon light, and peered out. From here she had nearly a bird's-eye view of the city. She could see the peaks of tents in Golden Gate Park and the plumes of smoke from fires just a few blocks to the east. What was happening in the Japanese Tea Garden right now?

Then she noticed a man and a woman walking slowly down her street. The man, limping heavily, leaned on the woman's arm. The woman wore a red dress!

Clara pressed against the dusty windowpane and strained to see better, but the couple turned the corner. *Goose!* she scolded herself. Lots of people wore red dresses! The man must have been injured in the quake like so many others, and he and his wife were probably heading for the park. Perhaps they had lost their home to the firebreak in the last explosion...

Clara carried the baby clothes downstairs. She glanced into the parlor and saw Father sitting at the broken front window in his chair, staring broodingly out into the street.

"Do you pray, Clara?" Father asked when he saw her. "If you do, then pray for rain. Only thing that can save our city now is rain."

Clara put one hand on Father's thin shoulder. It seemed to her the fires had been burning forever—for weeks, at least. Yet this was only the third day since the earthquake. So much had happened in a short time. She glanced at the mantle, then remembered that the clock had been smashed in the quake. "Father," she asked, "what is the time?"

He peered down at the pocket watch clipped to his vest. "Five-fifteen," he replied heavily.

"And Mr. Midgard and Mr. Stokes?"

"Still not returned," he said. "I hope there has been no trouble."

Clara felt heavy with dread.

She carried the box through the dining room, where Mr. Granger now sat at the table with the children and the Wheeler sisters, amazing them with card tricks. She took the box into the kitchen. Mother's eyes filled with tears as she searched through the tiny shirts and dresses. She held up a knitted blue sweater to show the other women at the kitchen table—she had made it herself, Clara knew, for Gideon when he was born—then pressed it to her heart. Clara looked away. Mother's grief was still so raw.

Finally Mother selected a few soft garments. She and Clara carried the baby outside. The air was thick with smoke and wind-borne ash. Mother placed the baby on a folded towel on the grass and stripped off the doll dress and the diaper.

Baby H gurgled and waved her fists. She really was a most engaging baby, Clara thought, and didn't seem to notice that her world was in crisis. Clara smiled down at the child, watching as Mother poured a small dipperful of warm water from the kettle into a bowl. "Here, dear." Mother held out the washcloth to Clara. "You'll be bathing your own babies someday, so why not learn now?"

Clara dunked the soft cloth into the water and wiped Baby H gently. The baby chuckled when Clara made silly faces. "Well done," Mother said. "I'll leave you to finish here and get her dressed again." Then Mother went back into the house.

As Clara leaned over the baby, pinning a clean folded diaper into place, her shoulder blades prickled. *I won't be like Edgar,* she told herself staunchly, *always imagining ghostly presences!* She knew full well that Mother had gone inside; Clara and the baby were alone in the backyard. She would *not* turn around.

She pulled a little dress that had once been her own — green cotton sprigged with white daisies — over the baby's head and struggled to get her arms through the armholes. Dressing a real baby was a lot harder than dressing Delilah! For one thing, Delilah lay nice and still, whereas Baby H was kicking her feet and wriggling as if she meant to jump up and run around ... cooing and laughing as if she were greeting her dearest friend ...

Clara's shoulder blades prickled again. She whirled around — and there was the woman in red. She was standing in the drive, watching. She looked battered and bruised, her left eye swollen shut.

Clara grabbed up the baby as the woman approached.

"Come here, sweet Helen, come to Hattie," cooed the woman. The baby laughed and stretched out her little arms.

"Get back!" shouted Clara. "I told you not to come here again!"

"Just give me the baby," the woman begged in a low, desperate voice. She held out her hands. "You don't understand! She's in terrible danger, and I am, too. I need to get her to her parents."

"You kidnapped her." Clara's voice was also low. She

tightened her grip on the baby. "I've figured it all out, so don't try to deny it! Her name is Helen Forrest, and you've kidnapped her from her parents in Oakland. You were seen boarding the ferry from Oakland—before the quake! I bet you panicked after the quake and left her here— and you've been trying to get her back so you can ask for ransom. Well, you're not having her! I'm going to see that she gets to Oakland myself—if Oakland hasn't burned to the ground as well!"

"*I'm* not the kidnapper!" gasped the woman, her voice trembling. "I'm Hattie Pitt, Helen's nursemaid. But if the kidnappers do get their ugly hands on her—" Her voice broke. "They're capable of anything. Oh, Lord, I never meant for any of this to happen!" She sank to the ground. Her shoulders heaved with sobs.

Edgar came out the back door and down the ramp to stand next to Clara. "Is that the kidnapper?" he whispered.

"I think so, though she says she's not," replied Clara tersely. The baby struggled in her arms and started to cry.

The woman—Hattie Pitt—lifted her head and reached for the child. "Shh, angel. Come to Hattie."

Edgar leaped between Clara and Hattie Pitt. "Nothing doing," he said. "Not till you've done your explaining."

"I saw you last night," Clara told her. "With that man— trying to break into our house! Father thought you were looters, but I know you came for the baby."

"Denny's no looter," Hattie said, shaking her head. "And he's not the kidnapper, either. And *you're* the one that hit him with the fireplace poker, you wretched girl! You broke his arm, do you know that? Then the Borden brothers broke his other one—" she sank to the ground, her shoulders shaking with silent sobs—"as punishment!"

Clara and Edgar exchanged a horrified look. Clara had not known she had the strength to break anyone's arm. She had acted on impulse, and out of fear. But— what had Hattie said about *punishment*? Who would deliberately set out to break a man's bones?

The baby was wailing now, a fretful wail that would soon bring Mother running out from the house. Clara thrust the baby into Edgar's arms and knelt next to Hattie in the grass. "I think you'd better come inside and tell us the whole story," Clara said sternly.

Hattie Pitt lifted her head and nodded vigorously. "Oh, yes," she said. "We must get Helen inside where no one can hear her." She struggled to her feet and reached for the baby. Edgar tightened his grip. Hattie stroked the baby's head with a trembling hand.

"Hush, my angel."

The back door opened and Mother came out to stand on the ramp. "Have you finished with the baby, Clara? Here, give her to me—" She broke off at the sight of Hattie. "You!"

"This is Hattie Pitt," said Clara succinctly.

"What's going on?" Mother demanded. "She's not taking that child!"

"No," agreed Clara. "She is coming inside to tell us her tale of woe. Not that I'll believe a word of it!"

Hattie looked up at them all with tragic eyes. "Whether you believe me or not," she whispered, "it's safer for the baby indoors. And I'm safer off the streets, too. I daren't be seen..."

Frowning, Mother led the way into the kitchen. Clara hurried to the parlor, where Miss Chandler and Miss DuBois were chatting with Mrs. Grissinger and Mrs. Hansen. Father still sat alone at the window. "Come into the kitchen, Father," she whispered into his ear. "The kidnapper is here!"

Father turned in surprise. Clara seized the handles of the wheelchair and spun it around. "She's come back," she told him in a low voice so the lodgers would not hear. "The lady in red!"

Clara, her parents, and Edgar sat around the kitchen table. Mother held the baby, letting her suck on a thick end of stale bread. Clearing her throat, Hattie began to speak. Clara frowned, listening for lies. But she had to admit to herself that Hattie sounded sincere.

Hattie Pitt was nineteen years old, she told them. Her mother was dead and her father was often away working on the railroad. She had raised her two younger brothers until they were old enough to get jobs for themselves.

Then she left home to take a position with the Forrests, who needed a nanny for their new baby girl.

Lucas and Roseanna Forrest lived in an imposing mansion in Oakland's most prestigious district. They were patrons of the arts, always attending art exhibits, plays, and especially the opera.

"They just love opera—" Hattie broke off as Clara cleared her throat loudly.

"What does all this have to do with kidnappers?" Clara demanded. "I don't get it."

"I'm working up to it," huffed Hattie.

"Now, dear girl," said Father gently, "let Miss Pitt tell the tale her own way."

Clara sat back and crossed her arms.

The Forrests had been invited to visit their friends, the Plumsteads, who lived on San Francisco's Nob Hill. Minnie Plumstead was a friend of Roseanna Forrest from their days as students at Mills College before their marriages. "Mrs. Forrest and Mrs. Plumstead—the two of them were crazy to hear some famous Italian fellow sing opera—Caruso, they said his name was."

"Enrico Caruso," nodded Father. "I've read about him. He's a famous Italian tenor. He was to perform for the first time in San Francisco just a few days ago."

"That's right," Hattie said eagerly. "So the Forrests took the ferry to San Francisco, leaving me minding Baby Helen. There were other servants at home, of course; we wouldn't be completely on our own. There was the cook, and the housekeeper..."

"But you brought the baby to San Francisco," prompted Clara. "You didn't stay home. *Why?*"

Hattie fingered her bruised cheek. "Because of Denny," she said softly. "Denny's my beau."

"Did he do that to you?" asked Father, pointing one finger to Hattie's battered face and black, swollen eye. "Did he beat you?"

"Denny'd never do a thing like that!" she replied indignantly. "It wasn't him! It was Sid."

"I'm getting confused!" complained Edgar. "Who's Sid?"

Mother just sat rocking the baby, rocking back and forth.

Hattie watched Mother in silence for a moment. When she spoke again, there was a catch in her voice. "Denny came to the Forrests' house. I was surprised, because I usually see him only on my day off."

Denny Dobson waited on tables at the elegant Cliff House, Hattie told them, where he rubbed shoulders with his upper-class patrons, and where he recently had come to the attention of two very dangerous men.

"Sid and Herman Borden," whispered Hattie. "Twin brothers, and the nastiest snakes you'd ever hope to meet. Not that we knew that then, of course! Denny liked them—said they were the toast of the town! Herman was the manager of the fancy Cliff House restaurant, and

his brother helped out. Or maybe it was the other way
around, with Sid the manager and Herman helping out.
I forget. Handsome fellows, anyway, always hobnobbing
with the society people—people like the Plumsteads, you
know, with big houses and fancy parties and the like.
Sometimes the Forrests would take me and Helen along
to these house parties. Of course we didn't really go as
guests, but I'd get glimpses, you know, of the dancing and
suchlike. Oh! It would be lovely to be rich!"

She broke off and touched her black eye, wincing.
Clara thought that Hattie must have other bruises as well,
ones they couldn't see.

"Yes, those twins are ever so elegant," Hattie murmured. "Look just the same, too, except for a long thin
scar across Sid's cheek. They were friendly to Denny out
at Cliff House … I guess he told them about how his
fiancée worked for the Forrests. Well, one night the
Borden brothers told Denny they had come up with a
great plan. No one would get hurt, and Denny would get
rich! Denny and me, we've been trying to save up to be
married, you know? We want to go to Alaska to settle.
You can get land cheap up there, you know …"

Again her voice trailed off.

Mother regarded Hattie with lips pursed in disap-
proval. "So it was a get-rich-quick scheme?" she asked.
"With this baby as bait?"

Hattie flushed. Her voice was very soft. "Denny came

to get me. He said we must bring Helen to a secret meeting with the Borden brothers. They promised no harm would come to the baby, and that we'd all end up rich as kings!"

"So you took the ferry to San Francisco," said Clara. "That's when you and Helen were 'last seen'—as it says in the poster."

"Denny took me to their lodgings," Hattie continued. She shook her head. "A dreadful place! Over by Chinatown, in a grubby shack ... I never would have imagined the elegant Borden brothers in such a place. I hated to take the baby inside, it was that dirty. Oh, they had fine things, no doubt about that. Paintings and sculptures and the like, and fancy carved furniture. But no fine house to put it all in, and no housekeeper to keep it in order. Denny and I sat there at their marble-topped table with dust on it an inch thick, and they told me their plan ..." Hattie's face grew chalky, her expression agitated. She reached over and traced one finger gently along Helen's cheek.

The plan was that the Borden twins would kidnap the baby and demand a high ransom from Roseanna and Lucas Forrest. Hattie sank her head into her hands. "I was horrified. I couldn't possibly let them have the baby. We argued about it all night. Denny promised no harm would come to little Helen, and that she would be home just as quickly as the parents forked over the money—which they have plenty of. They could afford it, Denny said, and then we'd take our cut of the ransom and settle in Alaska. I still said no. I told Denny he was crazy—but then I saw the gun in Sid's hand. Pointed right at Denny's heart. And I realized Denny had got in over his head."

Hattie's voice broke into a sob. "Herman had a revolver, too, pointed right at me and Helen. So in the end I had no choice but to do what they said—"

"Which was to disguise the baby," Clara said, and Hattie nodded. "I knew it!"

"They said she was too pretty in her lacy dress and bonnet," murmured Hattie. "Too memorable. 'Make her look like nobody's baby,' Sid ordered, and so I had to shave off Helen's beautiful brown curls and dress her in the dirty clothes they'd stolen off some beggar's child." Hattie wrapped her arms around herself as if for warmth. "It broke my heart to do it." She coughed in the smoky air. "And while I was doing that, they set Denny to cutting up newspapers, spelling out the demands of the ransom note to send up to the Plumsteads' mansion, where I'd told them the Forrests were staying."

"What did the note say?" asked Edgar eagerly.

"I didn't get a chance to read it," said Hattie. "Because right then everything started rattling and shaking—and it sounded like a train was rumbling right under the house and—oh, Lord, the whole room was bucking like some crazy old donkey!"

CHAPTER 10
THE PLOT

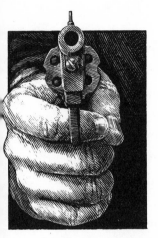

W*ho knows what was going on in any particular house when the earthquake hit?* Clara shivered, remembering Father's words.

"Everything was crazy then," cried Hattie. "The back wall of the Borden brothers' shack collapsed and shingles fell on our heads. A fire started in the kitchen and came roaring at us—we all got out in the nick of time. I had Helen in my arms, and Sid Borden had my shoulder in an iron grip—and Herman had Denny, and they towed us through the streets to a back-alley carriage house. We hid there with the baby for ages, it seemed, until we started hearing people racing past on the street, saying that the whole city was on fire—Chinatown, the East Side, even Nob Hill! 'Even the Plumstead Mansion?' Herman worried. So Sid sent him out to check. Later Herman returned with the news that the Plumstead mansion had collapsed and all the people inside were dead.

"'Damnation!' Sid snarled. 'So who is left to pay ransom for the kid?' Herman said, 'Nobody, and now we're stuck with this mewling brat!'

"Sid yelled that the Borden brothers are never stuck! And he grabbed Helen right out of my arms and shoved her into Denny's. 'Get rid of it,' he said, as cold as you please."

Hattie clenched her hands in front of her on the tabletop. "'What do you mean, *get rid of it*?' I shouted."

"'Dump it—so it can't be traced to us,' ordered Herman, and they sent Denny at gunpoint into the streets."

Hattie shuddered. "I couldn't let it happen. I was screaming like a banshee, and Sid slapped me hard, but I ran out after Denny and the baby...and another tremor knocked us to our knees..."

Hattie gasped for breath. Clara felt her own heart beating hard. She could picture how it must have been, with Hattie running through the smoke and chaos after Denny.

"We escaped!" rasped Hattie. "But we had no money and no place to go, and what were we going to do with this orphaned baby? I knew she had grandparents over in Oakland—but we couldn't get to the Ferry Building because of the fires. We heard that people were being sent to Golden Gate Park for safety, so we headed that way, too. Oh, we walked for blocks and blocks, up and down so many hills, and everywhere were homeless people crying and looking for their lost loved ones . . . and then I saw your house. It seemed calmer here—and I thought this would be a safe place to leave the baby. I snuck into the back and took the quilt and the laundry basket and tucked little Helen in. She was asleep by then, poor lamb, worn out from so many frights . . ."

"And we know the rest," said Mother. She reached over and patted Hattie's hand comfortingly. "It seems you saved the baby's life."

Clara glanced over at Mother sharply. "After endangering her in the first place!"

Hattie looked down at Mother's hand resting on hers. "I'm afraid—"

"Who wouldn't have been afraid, dear?"

Clara cleared her throat. "I suspect there's more to the story, Mother."

"The Borden brothers, right?" demanded Edgar.

"I'm afraid so," said Hattie. "When Herman and Sid saw the posters that said the Forrests were searching for me and the baby, they were livid. They realized that even though the Plumsteads' house had collapsed and burned, somehow the Forrests were still alive. No doubt the Forrests rushed home to Oakland on the first possible ferry after the quake struck, only to find their baby girl missing. The housekeeper over in Oakland had seen me heading for the ferry before the quake, so she must have reported that to the parents, and they hurried back to

San Francisco. When the Borden brothers read the posters, they decided to get their kidnapping plan back on track.

"They found me and Denny in the park and told us to get the baby back. When I refused, they beat us up. So I came here—and I tried, you know I tried! But you sent me away, and I couldn't blame you, really. And then Sid and Herman sent me and Denny here at night. We were supposed to break in and snatch Helen... But that didn't work, either."

Clara winced, remembering the dull thud of the heavy iron poker on Denny's arm and his howl of pain. But she had kept Helen safe that night, without even knowing the danger awaiting her.

"Wait a minute," Clara interrupted. "Why didn't you and Denny just run off together, leaving the baby with us? That way, when we saw the poster, *we'd* be the ones to take her back to her parents in Oakland. The two of you would be safely gone to Alaska, and the baby would be safe with us!"

"You still don't understand," Hattie protested. "The baby *isn't* safe with you. She'll *never* be safe here. Sid and Herman beat us both up something terrible when we came back without the baby—Denny worse than me— he's still unconscious! I hated to leave him, but I had to try to save Helen. Sid and Herman have vowed to capture Helen themselves. Sid wrote that note asking you to meet

him at the Japanese Tea Garden and made me slip it under
the door. But you didn't go—I'm glad you didn't!—and
they'll be truly furious now."

"Oh, dear Mr. Midgard and Mr. Stokes," murmured
Mother. "I'm so desperately sorry if we've sent them into
trouble!"

"Sid and Herman will kill me if they find me here,"
moaned Hattie. "But I had to come. I wanted to take
Helen to the police while the Bordens were waiting at the
tea garden. Her parents must be frantic, and I must try to
right the wrongs I've done. If anything happens to Helen,
it will be on my conscience forever!"

"On yours *and* mine," declared Mother. She kissed
Baby Helen's bristly head. "I thought it was Providence
who brought this baby to us. The Lord working in mysterious ways, you know."

Father reached over and patted Mother's shoulder
awkwardly. Clara was surprised and pleased to see this;
it had been a very long time since her parents had touched
each other. Since before the accident, she guessed.

"But you understand far too well," he said in his deep
voice, "about losing a child."

"Oh, I do," she whispered.

And with a sweep of memory Clara was back in time
to those two stormy days after the shipwreck when they
didn't know whether Father and Gideon would be found...
whether father and son had been smashed on the rocks

along with the steamship or whether they had somehow made it to shore along with the several crewmen who had been pulled from the wreckage ... Clara remembered how time seemed to stand still while she and Mother didn't know, how every breath hurt and there was a terrible ache inside her instead of a heartbeat.

This was how Roseanna and Lucas Forrest felt now. All the wealth in the world wouldn't shield them from the pain of losing their baby girl, and Mother understood this.

"So of course Helen must be returned," Mother said resolutely. "We had best go for the police right now." She stood up with the baby in her arms. "This minute."

Clara pushed back her chair. "I'm coming with you," she said.

"Me too!" said Edgar, his eyes shining with excitement.

"Oh, no," said Mother. "You two will stay here. Clara especially. Am I to lose first Gideon, then Helen—and you, too?" She put her hands on her hips. "Oh, no. You will stay home and stay *safe*—"

"I won't be safe if the Borden brothers come here looking for Helen, Mother!"

Father cleared his throat. Clara looked at him in irritation, sure he would say, as he always said, *Mother knows best.*

But he spoke to his wife. "Alice," he said firmly, "I think you shall remain here."

Mother's voice was sharp. "Frederick! The telephones

are out of order, and we must get the baby to the police *now*."

Father shook his head. "In this confusion? Alice, I forbid it. The whole city is afire, people are homeless and injured, everything lies in ruins—and you think the police will be sitting at the station to take care of this baby?"

Mother's expression was determined. "I simply must keep this child safe, and that is my final word on the matter."

Father stared at her, then slumped into his chair in defeat. It hadn't been much of a fight, really, Clara thought. But it was more spunk than he'd shown in two years. Before the accident there would have been no question. When Father put his foot down, his word was law. He had been captain of his ship, head of his household, and final authority over his children ... until off they'd sailed, with Mother's prayers for safe passage ringing in their ears.

At least Father tried, Clara told herself. But it wasn't enough. It never was with Mother, anymore. Gideon's death hung between them—*and it always, always will.*

Mother handed the baby to Hattie and reached for her shawl on the peg by the back door. "We shall leave right now," she said. "Clara, you and Edgar shall serve the lodgers their dinner."

Clara clenched her hands into fists. She felt like screaming at her mother, but she held herself in check.

"Wait. You ought to return this with the baby." She reached into her pocket and withdrew the silver rattle.

Mother stowed the rattle in her own pocket, then sailed out the door with Hattie following.

Baby Helen's head bobbed on Hattie's shoulder and her wide brown gaze looked back at Clara. *Good-bye,* the baby seemed to be saying. *Pray for safe passage.*

CHAPTER 11
KIDNAPPED!

Clara and Edgar looked anxiously at each other until Father cleared his throat. "Alice is a determined woman," he said. "But I should have put my foot down."

"Shall I go after them, Father?" asked Clara.

He considered her. "Yes, do that. Run as fast as you can, and tell Mother I *insist* that she return. We will hide the baby here until morning. Surely Mr. Stokes and Mr. Midgard will have returned by then to help guard her. It is madness to go out into these conditions at night."

"I'll run like the wind!" Clara jumped to her feet as Mr. Granger and the Wheeler sisters appeared in the kitchen looking for their dinner. "Coming, Edgar?"

"You bet!"

"Hurry, children. But if they won't stop, I want you to return. Don't linger in the streets. Do you understand?"

Clara nodded. "Yes, Father."

"I will keep your supper warm, children."

"Now where are those young ones off to?" wondered Mr. Granger.

Clara left Father to answer. She and Edgar were out the door and running down the street. The air was cooler than it had been and the sky was thick with bits of ash swirling in the wind. Clara coughed as she ran. Mother and Hattie must have turned the corner already; there was no sign of them.

"Come on," cried Clara. "They can't have gotten far." She ran around the corner with Edgar at her heels. She'd thought the wound on her foot had healed, but running made it ache again. She tried to ignore it as she leaped over piles of rubble and darted around people and their makeshift shelters at the sides of the roads.

It would be about ten blocks to the police station. But maybe Clara would find a policeman along the way. Where could Mother and Hattie be? Surely they couldn't have come much farther than this so quickly?

"Wrong way, young'uns," a man told them as he pushed past on the next block. "You want to head for the park. Everything's gone up ahead. Everything's in ruins!"

"They must be taking the side streets," Clara said to Edgar when, after another block, they still had not found Mother and Hattie.

"Zigzagging through the streets to throw the kidnappers off," he added, a note of excitement in his voice.

Clara didn't answer. The closer they got to Market Street, the more misery they saw. It looked like the end of the world had come. Ash swirled in the wind. Burned pages from books flew past and crunched under their feet as they walked along. It was hard to tell which buildings and houses had been destroyed by the quake and which by fire—everything around them was leveled to piles of stone and brick, all blackened with soot, some still smoldering. Refugees streamed in all directions, some heading toward Golden Gate Park, some toward the ferries that would take them away from the hell that had been their shining city. And over everything hung an unearthly hush. Clara heard none of the ordinary city sounds—no jangle of tram bells or clatter of carriages. No whistle from deliverymen making their rounds. No call of paperboys: *Evening edition, hot off the press!* Only silence. A wounded quiet.

"Maybe we should turn back, do you think?" asked Clara. "What if the police station is gone, too?" She hated to think they had come this far without finding Mother and Hattie and the baby. But the scene around them was so much more terrible than what she'd seen in her own neighborhood, she felt helpless and frightened.

"There they are!" yelled Edgar suddenly, grabbing Clara's arm. "Up ahead!"

Up the block, Clara caught a glimpse of Mother and Hattie just disappearing over the crest of the hill. "Mother!" shouted Clara. "Hattie! Wait for us!" She and Edgar started running.

The sky darkened, and there was a rumble that at first Clara thought must be another house exploding for the firebreak. Then she realized that the rumbling came from overhead. *Thunder!* The sound of thunder was rare in San Francisco. Rain usually just *fell,* unaccompanied by thunder and lightning. *"Rain!"* Clara shouted.

"Just what we needed three days ago!" Edgar shouted in reply.

The rain pattered down in a soothing shower, wetting the ash and clearing the evening air. Up ahead of them, Mother and Hattie had stopped and were waiting. Mother stood with hands on hips. Her scowl looked most forbidding. Hattie, holding the baby wrapped in Mother's shawl, bent low to shield Helen from the rain.

"I told you to stay home, young lady," Mother said as Clara approached. "I will not let you risk your safety, and I will not stand for disobedience!"

"Wait, Mother, please listen." Clara put out her hand. "Father sent us. As soon as you left, he told us to run after you. He insists you return—"

Mother stared at Clara. "He said that?" She hesitated, then shook her head and resumed walking. "We have come so far already. And our first concern must be for this baby."

"But, Mother, wait. Father says we'll hide Helen at our house, and she'll be safe until things settle down again and we can take her safely and easily—"

Mother slowed. "He said all that?" Then she snorted. "Longest speech in two years—and I missed it?"

"He did say all that, ma'am," Edgar piped up. "Indeed, he seemed terribly anxious."

For a moment, Mother's expression softened. She glanced over at Hattie and Helen. They were a sorry sight, soaked through in the pouring rain. A woman on horseback sloshed past them in the gutter, soiled bundles piled on the horse's back making her look like a disreputable peddler, though she had probably been a respectable housewife only days before.

Other people passed them, heading for the park—even a leaky tent would be better than nothing at all . . . And then Clara saw out of the corner of her eye two people coming the other way—away from the park, as she herself had come: two men approaching silently up the hill, marching side by side together—then, as they reached the crest, splitting up to walk several yards apart. They might have been soldiers patrolling for looters. They might have been everyday citizens out for a walk in the rain. But as they drew closer, Clara saw their faces set in identical expressions of determination. In fact, the faces were perfectly identical altogether, except for the scar scoring the cheek of the man on the left . . .

"Run!" she screeched as the men closed in on Hattie and the baby. "It's the kidnappers!"

With a shriek, Hattie turned to flee, but the man with the scar spun her around, knocking her to the ground. Edgar launched himself at the man, kicking him hard in the back as he tried to wrest the baby from Hattie's arms.

"You've betrayed us once too often, Hattie my dear," Clara heard the man growl. "You've been a very bad girl."

Baby Helen's wails rose above the sound of the rain. Mother, held around the middle by the other twin, screamed for the police.

As the man with the scar twisted around to punch Edgar, Clara saw her chance. She darted forward and snatched the baby, then started running back down the hill at top speed.

Her skirts swirled around her and the wind slapped rain against her face. *Don't let me fall, don't let me fall,* Clara prayed, hugging Helen to her chest.

Her feet pounded the cracked paving stones. Her heel throbbed with her heartbeat. She headed back toward the streets where the homeless had erected their blanket tents. The kidnappers would not attack with witnesses all around, would they?

She rounded the corner, slowing down as much as she dared so that she would not slip on the slick stones. *Hush, hush,* she whispered to the baby. The baby's cries were a siren in the dusk, announcing their presence. She listened for the sound of footsteps behind her, but heard nothing. She'd made it! She'd taken the baby and escaped!

Panting now from exertion, Clara slowed her pace. How many more blocks till she would be home? Too many—she'd better start zigzagging through the streets to make it harder for the men to track her. Somehow she would get home—she *had* to!—and somehow they'd hide this baby until the police could be summoned. Surely Mother and Hattie and Edgar would follow. *Oh, please, don't let the kidnappers hurt them...*

The rainy street was deserted except for Clara and Baby Helen. And—except for the motorcar chugging down the hill behind them.

Almost home, almost home...

The motorcar stopped. Two figures jumped out. Police? Soldiers? Clara peered through the rain in a panic and realized that *almost home* was not good enough.

The men closed in on her. She fought like a mother seal protecting her pup: bellowing for help, lashing out with her whole body, bending tight to hold little Helen, who howled in terror.

The rain slashed down. "Let go, brat!" snarled a voice in her ear as iron-strong arms pried the baby from her grip.

Clara struggled to hang on to Helen. When she lost the struggle, she clawed at her attackers' faces. "I've seen you!" she screamed at them. "I know your faces! I'll turn you over to the police and you'll be sorry!"

The man who had Helen cursed. "You hear her, Sid?"

"Just take 'em both," the other man growled over the wailing and the rain. "Just get 'em in the auto and *go*!"

Something coarse and heavy was slapped around Clara's head, something pulled tight, nearly cutting off light and breath. She felt herself being lifted, tossed like a bag of coal into the air...Then a brutal blow, and pain exploding behind her ears...

And darkness.

Chapter 12
ON THE ROCKS

She was struggling to swim. The dark figure below her was tangled in seaweed. She battled the water, her body stiff and slow...

Clara awoke slowly, head groggy, mouth dry and stuffed with something fuzzy. Her body felt heavy, cold and wet. She lay on a gritty surface, roughness under her cheek. She opened her eyes, wincing at the pain that stabbed behind them. She reached up to tug off the strip of cloth that gagged her. It was fabric she recognized as having come from her own skirt. She could see the cornflower pattern in the moonlight.

Yes, it was night. Clara could see now that she was lying on a slab of rock. Darkness surrounded her. She could hear the sound of rain but, strangely, it was not falling on her. She looked up into blackness. There was no sky overhead—just inky rock. She seemed to be inside a sort of cave. She closed her eyes slowly, trying to remember.

She had lost the baby. She had been taken by the kidnappers and left—where? She sniffed. The night air smelled like salt.

Over the patter of the rain she could hear a sound that frightened her almost as much as the kidnappers had because it was so unexpected: the sound of waves breaking on rocks below her.

Moving slowly to keep the dizziness at bay, she inched forward and peered over the edge of the cave. Her head pounded from the blow that had knocked her unconscious, but the sick feeling in her stomach came from the sight before her.

Waves surged among sharp rocks only a few feet below the edge of the cave. She craned her neck around the cave opening, gasping at the pain in her head. To her right, more rock, and the dark rise of hills in the distance. To her left … Clara blinked. Incredibly, she knew this place. She could see the dome of the Sutro Baths.

Clara shivered. The kidnappers had stashed her in a cave in an outcropping of rocks very near Seal Rocks, where Father's steamship had wrecked. Where Gideon had died.

She had not been near this area since the dreadful day after the accident, when she and Mother watched while rescue crews searched for survivors. Now here she was, back again.

Now *she* was a survivor.

The Borden brothers had not killed her, and she was grateful, of course. But she wondered if the kidnappers were stupid men. They hadn't killed her, and they hadn't even tied her up! Yes, she'd been rendered unconscious, but surely the men must realize that as soon as she woke up and climbed out of the cave, she would go for the police!

She gasped in shock as a spray of cold water splashed her face. Struggling, she peered over the edge again. Rain pelted her head. The tide was coming in swiftly and waves were lapping very close to the mouth of the cave. The sharp rocks were covered now by the dark, salty ocean. Soon the cave would be filled—and the kidnappers must have known that. Not stupid after all, then—just evil to the bone. *They mean for me to die out here!* The terrible knowledge that she might not have regained consciousness in time gave Clara new strength. She must escape now—or perish.

Pushing away the dizzy feeling, she scrambled to her knees and slung her feet over the edge of the cave opening. She would have to walk along rocks underwater now until she could climb onto safer ground. She struggled out of the cave, gasping as freezing water closed around her ankles. She clung to the rock face and edged along, carefully feeling her way. The wind blew rain and sea spray into her eyes, and she shook her head, not daring to let go of the rock to wipe her face. Would she ever see Mother and Father again?

Clara!

She froze, listening. The kidnappers? Or someone coming to help her?

Hold on! the voice cried, and she realized with a shock that the voice pounded inside her own head. *Hold on tight, Old Sock!*

"Oh, no, Gideon!" she muttered through teeth clenched against the cold. "I will surely lose my grip if I see a ghost now!—and I don't believe in ghosts anyway!" She wondered if the crack on the head had made her delirious.

The toes of her sodden high-button shoes scrabbled hard against the rock as she climbed out of the water. She grasped knobs of sea-worn rock, found little footholds in hollows. Then she heard another voice—a high-pitched cry coming from up above. *Baby Helen?* Had the men stashed the baby inside another cave, meaning to leave them *both* to drown?

You monsters, thought Clara furiously. "I'm coming, Helen!" she shouted, peering up into the falling rain. But all she saw were two screeching seagulls glaring down from their roost on the rocks above. They opened their beaks and shrieked at her. Not the baby, then, after all.

At last she reached level ground and rested on the rocks, panting and shivering in the rain. The hulking mass of the Sutro Baths was shrouded in darkness. The huge panels of glass over the domed baths must have shattered in the earthquake. She rounded the building and picked her way cautiously toward higher ground, toward the pathway leading up to Sutro Heights and out to the road. She had to find help.

She had to find Helen.

The rain slackened as she squelched along, shivering in her wet clothing, heading toward the road. In the distance, beyond the baths, she could make out a light. It must come from Cliff House, she decided, which might mean that the imposing building had not been too badly damaged in the earthquake. She knew that it would probably be a long time before people returned to the exhibitions, restaurants, and art galleries at Cliff House, but no matter. There was a light, and that might mean shelter and help on this dreadful night.

Now the rain stopped altogether. Clouds overhead began to part as Clara raced along the path. She moved as quickly as she dared with only the moon lighting her way. *Satchel to Cliff House.* The words echoed in her mind. Had it been the kidnappers' plan all along to bring Helen here? What would Clara find once she reached that lighted room?

She slowed her steps. Cliff House loomed in front of her like a fortress. Were shelter and safety to be found there—or danger?

From the side of the path came a rustling noise. Then

a hand shot out from the bushes and grabbed her arm. Clara's scream split through the night and sent gulls screeching overhead in alarm.

"Shh," hissed a voice at her side. "It's me!" Edgar emerged from the bushes, scratched and dirty and looking more like a ragamuffin than ever by moonlight. But Clara had never been so glad to see anybody in her life and she wrapped her arms around him in a great hug.

"Get off!" he muttered, struggling out of her grip. "Thank goodness you're all right!"

"Where's Helen?" she asked, relief at seeing him turning to dismay as he shook his head.

"*You* had her, last I saw," he said.

Clara's eyes filled with tears. She blinked them back. "The men knocked me unconscious and left me on the rocks to drown. I escaped, but I didn't see Helen—"

Edgar pulled her off the path. They knelt behind the bushes that formed a screen between them and the palatial Cliff House. "At least *you're* safe," he said huskily. "That's something."

"How did you know to look for me here anyway?" she asked, staring at him in confusion.

"I didn't know for sure," Edgar said in a low voice, "but the paper you'd found with the baby said something about Cliff House. It was the only clue, so I told the police. I *had* to try to find you." He shifted in the bushes. "I mean, you've been helping me out, so it's only right..."

"You mean the police know we're here?" whispered Clara. "Well, where are they then? We've got to find Helen!"

Edgar sounded puzzled. "I haven't seen anybody— though I was sure they'd be here. Maybe they're still looking after your mother—"

"Mother is hurt?" cried Clara. "Edgar, tell me what happened!"

"Sshh!" He glanced around nervously. "You ran off, and those men knocked your mother to the ground and took off after you. Your mother had a gash on her fore- head, and Hattie stayed with her while I ran for the cops. By the time I found one, blood was streaming down your mother's face, but all she could talk about was how you'd rescued the baby and she was so proud of you ... It wasn't till the cop found a cart and driver to carry us back to your house that we all realized you and Helen never made it home. Your parents were frantic."

Clara could imagine. And no doubt Mother would somehow blame Father for this calamity, too. She felt a terrible urgency to be out of these bushes, to be searching for Baby Helen. But Edgar was chattering on, relating his account of events, and she could hear the same nervous note of shock in his voice that she'd noticed that first day in the park.

"Yeah, your parents were crazy, and the cop was all upset, too, because he'd counted on finding you and the baby there! See, he said, the Forrests' housekeeper had come to the station to report that they'd received a ransom note. The note said to bring a suitcase of money directly to Cliff House at midnight if they ever wanted to see their baby again! Then the cops came straight to the park to tell the parents, and they all went back to the police station."

"You mean the Forrests were right there at the police station while we were fighting off the Borden brothers?"

"Exactly," Edgar said. "And once I told the cop about the note with the baby, he wanted to get back to the station right away to get the Forrests and head out for Cliff House. Hattie was going with him, and I wanted to, too. But—can you believe this?—the cop just thanked me for my help and told me to stay with your parents!"

He snorted—a loud sound in the quiet darkness. "The cop said, 'Stay where you're safe, lad! We'll find them ourselves!'" Edgar sniffed. "Well, soon as they left for the station, I took your bicycle from the shed and made my way here on my own." He shook his head. "Sure was hard, though, with the road all torn up from the quake." He reached into the middle of the thicket. "See? Your bike's stashed right here."

Clara didn't care about the bicycle; she cared about the baby. She glanced around uneasily into the darkness that surrounded them. "So you think everybody's hiding around here somewhere, waiting for midnight?"

"Yup—the police, the Forrests, Hattie—maybe my

old Uncle James to boot!" Clara could see Edgar's nervous grin in the moonlight. "We surely lead an exciting life, don't we?"

Clara reached for his hand in the darkness, and he did not pull away. "Listen," she said, "if we knew where the police and the Forrests were hiding, we could go to them. But we *don't* know where they are, or even if they're really here." Surely every officer on the force was needed for fighting fires and halting looters and helping the injured. How many policemen could be spared to stake out Cliff House at midnight? She and Edgar didn't even have a pocket watch to tell them when it was midnight. "We can't just stand here," she told Edgar. "We've got to search for that poor baby!"

"Not a *poor* baby—she's *rich!*" Edgar corrected, his voice giddy.

"So she is," Clara retorted, "and that's how this whole mess began." Then without another word, she darted off down the path as fast as her shaky legs would allow, keeping to the shadows. The light inside Cliff House drew her like a beacon.

"Clara, wait!" Edgar hissed behind her.

But she did not stop. There was no time for waiting.

CHAPTER 13
SHOWDOWN AT CLIFF HOUSE

Clara hurried on, with Edgar right behind. The towering bulk of Cliff House loomed above them in the darkness, lit only by the glow in one window.

It was a spectacular building, an eight-story gingerbread mansion with four corner towers and a center steeple rising up into the moonlight. The house was decorated with crenellations and spires like a castle. Clara had been there several times with her family and on school trips, sitting out on the balcony where, for a dime, you could look out at the magnificent view for as long as you liked, eating ice cream from the concession stands. Inside, people enjoyed afternoon tea in the parlors, drinks in the bars, wedding receptions in the lunchrooms, dances in the ballroom, and tours through the art gallery. Those who could afford to dined in the fine restaurant—where, Clara remembered, Edgar's Uncle James had worked. And where Denny, Hattie's boyfriend, had first met the Borden brothers.

During the daytime the roiling ocean, the towering cliffs, and the barking seals out on Seal Rocks presented visitors to Cliff House with amazing views. It had always felt like an elegant, friendly place to Clara. But now, at night, Cliff House did not feel the least bit friendly. Clara and Edgar crept together along the pathway at the side until they were standing just under the ground-floor window that shone with flickering yellow light.

Clara breathed into Edgar's ear, "I wish we knew who was in there."

"Boost me up," whispered Edgar. "I'll peek inside. And maybe I can open it."

"Whoever's in there didn't go in by the window," Clara whispered back. "Let's try the doors."

"This place feels like Dracula's castle," murmured Edgar, glancing over his shoulder as they tried first one basement door, then another. "Gives me the creeps."

Clara was shivering hard as she tugged on the handle of the third basement door. The huge door yielded to her hands, and she edged it open. "All right, we're in!" She beckoned to Edgar, who crept after her into darkness.

They had to wait a moment for their eyes to adjust to the lack of moonlight. They were in a long hallway; this they could make out by the faint light that flickered through the window of the closed door on their right.

Tall white letters were painted on it: OFFICE. Clara pressed herself against the wall and sidled along until she reached the door. She could hear murmuring. Deep voices.

Fear coursed through her like a wave. Her hands felt clammy. Her wet clothes stuck to her like a cold second skin. She knew who was in there: the Borden brothers. The men who had injured her mother, overpowered Clara, ripped the baby from her arms, knocked Clara unconscious. The men who had carried her to the rocks and left her in the cave to drown.

Now they were waiting for their ransom money. But was the baby with them?

Clara wished she knew what time it was. She wished she knew for sure that the police were nearby. *Where is everybody?* she thought desperately.

Edgar crept closer to the office door. "This hallway is so dark," he whispered. "I bet they can't tell we're out here." He peeked through the door's window.

Clara held her breath and moved forward so she could see, too. She stifled a scream at the sight of the two kidnappers only a few feet away. One was seated at a large wooden desk with his feet propped casually on a pile of papers. The other—Sid, the one with the jagged scar—lounged in a leather armchair facing the big window wall. What a good thing Edgar hadn't tried to climb up to look into the window—illumined by moonlight, he would have been seen by the men for sure! Clara's heart thudded at the thought.

There was no sign of Denny. But there on the desk next to Herman's booted feet lay a bundle wrapped in Mother's shawl. A bundle that lay frighteningly still. Clara could barely draw breath. Was Helen dead? Had these monsters killed her?

Clara and Edgar waited for what seemed like hours, hovering silently outside the office door, keeping watch through the glass. The lamplight flickered. The kidnappers chatted to each other in voices so low that Clara could make out only a murmur. Herman tapped his long fingers restlessly on the desktop and checked his watch. Sid rose several times and walked to the window to stare outside. Then he sat back in the armchair.

Clara figured the baby *couldn't* be dead. Why would the men just be sitting around with a dead body on the desk, she asked herself wildly. That wouldn't make sense. But if Helen was alive—why was she lying so deathly still?

Hang on, Old Sock.

The thought filtered into Clara's head as if Gideon had spoken. She felt obscurely comforted, though she knew it must be just her imagination. She wished he were here with her, though. Gideon always knew what to do next.

She and Edgar jumped away from the door when they heard the chug of an automobile outside. *Help is here!* Clara thought gladly, but Edgar hissed, "Hide!" And so they darted down the long hallway and crouched in the deep shadows of a stairwell. Peering out, they could see the basement door opening. A young man wearing a dark suit and bowler hat stepped inside. He held a lantern. In the pale light they could see that he carried a satchel.

It's not the police, Clara realized. Could it be Denny? Or—could it be Lucas Forrest, the baby's father, arriving at midnight as the ransom note had specified? Clara watched from the shadows as the man set the satchel down just inside the basement door. Then he slowly moved outside again, letting the door close behind him.

Isn't he even going to look for his baby? wondered Clara. She couldn't understand it. She wanted to run after him, grab his arm and make him come to the office to rescue little Helen. She actually took a step forward, but Edgar pulled her back.

None too soon, because the office door opened and there was Sid—or was it Herman? Too dark to see a scar—but whoever it was held a revolver. The man strolled casually into the hallway.

Clara pushed herself hard against the wall. She had the most oppressive feeling of danger, as if a heavy weight were pressing down on her. She prayed he would not look their way; she prayed that the shadows would hide them.

Then, with a grunt of satisfaction, he grabbed the satchel and turned back to the office.

It was several minutes after the door closed behind him that Clara and Edgar dared to edge back down the hallway to peer through the office door. Clara gasped at the sight of the two triumphant men gleefully stashing wads of money into their pockets and coats. The satchel stood open on the desk next to the baby.

There must be a way to get that baby away from the men. Clara felt desperation rise in her, and a terrible longing to burst into tears. The shock of the earthquake, the fear of fire—these were nothing compared to the terror she felt now. Earthquake and fire were forces of nature. But the ruthlessness and greed of men who would stop at nothing—these were the forces of calculated evil. Clara bit the inside of her cheeks, willing herself not to make a sound. She couldn't overpower the men; she had found that out already. But when they left, perhaps she could follow them.

Or would it be better to leave *now*, while the men were busy with the money, and try to find the police? But what if the police weren't anywhere out there at all?

Clara's thoughts were in a whirl, but one thing was certain. She would never leave Baby Helen with the kidnappers.

Then Clara heard a little sound outside the basement door. A tiny scrape. A footstep. And then the creak of the door…opening just a crack.

She and Edgar pressed back into the shadows. Clara could feel Edgar trembling against her. Had the kidnappers heard? But, no, a bark of laughter came from the office. And then one of the men blew out the lamp.

The office door opened and the kidnappers stepped into the hallway. Was the baby with them? It was too dark to see without the light.

But suddenly there *was* light—as the basement door burst open and two policemen stepped into the hallway, revolvers drawn. Behind them stood the man in the bowler hat, lantern held high.

"Halt! Police!"

"Hey!" shouted Sid—or was it Herman?—in furious surprise. The other twin, quicker than his brother, turned to run down the hallway, right past Clara and Edgar. Clara saw that he was clutching the baby. Helen's head lolled sideways.

"She's dead," breathed Clara, and she knew that she and Edgar would probably be next. The shadows wouldn't hide them now.

"Not dead," whispered Edgar as the baby let out a little moan. "Drugged!"

"Stop right there or we'll shoot," ordered the older officer, pointing his gun at the men.

"Not with this baby in my arms, you won't," snarled the man holding Helen. Clara could see Sid's scar quite plainly now. He and his brother edged down the hallway, away from the police, toward the children's hiding place in the stairwell.

"Hey!" shouted Sid, as Clara caught her breath. "It's the girl! How'd she get away?"

"You should have killed her while we had the chance," hissed Herman, his eyes flicking toward Clara.

She almost choked at the menace of his cold gaze.

The police officers leveled their revolvers at the men. "What are these kids doing here?" yelled one policeman.

"Keep out of the line of fire!" his deputy barked to Clara and Edgar.

"Hand over my baby!" the man in the bowler hat cried to the kidnappers. "You've got your money—what more do you want?"

"We want our freedom," said Sid grimly. Helen moaned again, and Sid clamped a big palm roughly over her face.

"We told you to come alone, Forrest," Herman snarled. "But you broke our deal, and now you'll pay the price."

"And the price is that you don't get the brat back," Sid added. Using the baby as a shield, the two men sauntered past the police and Lucas Forrest, down the hallway, and out the basement door.

As the door closed behind them, the baby let out a wail that broke Clara's heart. The policemen and Mr. Forrest burst out of the building after the kidnappers, and Clara and Edgar followed. The police ordered the children to stay back, then pelted after the men. Clara and Edgar, keeping to shadows, rounded the side of Cliff House and followed the running figures heading down to Ocean Beach. Clara slipped in the sand and fell to her knees.

Gasping for breath, she stared at the action down on shore. She could just make out a tiny rowboat in the shallows. The dark shape of a larger vessel waited farther offshore.

"They've got accomplices," Edgar grunted, pulling Clara to her feet again.

"Stop them!" yelled Lucas Forrest in desperation, his voice breaking. "They're taking my daughter!" He and the policemen raced across the sand as the kidnappers sloshed out to the rowboat and tossed the baby inside. They struggled to launch it into the waves as the police-men aimed their revolvers.

Don't shoot! Clara prayed. *You might hit Helen!*

The kidnappers leaped into the boat with the baby. Rowing hard, they headed toward the larger boat—a fish-ing boat, Clara could tell—that was anchored offshore.

"You've bungled this!" howled Mr. Forrest in helpless fury, shaking the deputy's arm. "I took your advice, and look what's happened! You must go after them! You've got to stop them!"

Shots cracked into the night as the deputy fired a warning into the air.

Fury welled up inside Clara, and she couldn't hold back any longer. "Shooting won't help!" she shouted at the policemen. And without thinking of her own safety, she dashed past them to the edge of the water. "Stop!" she screamed out at the kidnappers. "You don't need the baby! Give Helen back!"

One of the men, only a dark shape now in the bobbing boat, fired his revolver toward the beach. The policeman dragged Clara back from the water. "It's no use, young lady. You'll get yourself shot."

They all watched helplessly from shore as the rowboat reached the larger fishing vessel. Shadowy men leaned down to haul the kidnappers into the boat. The fishing boat, canvas sails snapping in the wind, raised its anchor and disappeared around the treacherous Seal Rocks, leaving the small rowboat bobbing on choppy waves.

Then all they could hear was the thin, heartbreaking wail of the baby over the sound of the surf.

CHAPTER 14
PERIL AT SEA

They've left her in the boat!" shouted Lucas Forrest. "Thank the Lord!" But the little rowboat was moving quickly in the treacherous current and Clara knew it would soon be dashed on the rocks.

She steeled herself against the terrible cold and plunged straight into the water. Her skirt, already torn by the kidnappers to make the gag that had bound her mouth, ripped easily under her frantic hands now as she struggled to free her legs. She was a strong swimmer; that was one thing in her favor. She and Gideon used to race each other across the pools in the Sutro Baths, and she would emerge the victor at least half the time. He had taught her well.

Clara told herself she had a fifty-fifty chance of reaching the baby—although this swim was fearfully different from a swim at the baths. The current was strong, the water was frigid, and the biting cold took her breath away. She

spat out salty water and kicked harder, desperate to reach
the rowboat before the rowboat reached the rocks. She
could hear the people on shore shouting to her, but whether
they were urging her on or demanding her return, she
could not tell.

*She streaked through the waves like a sleek gray seal. "I'm
coming!" she cried to the figure struggling in the water...*

The cold was bone-numbing. Clara peered ahead in
the darkness. She was nowhere near the rocks yet, and not
nearly close enough to the boat. Each time she struck out
her arms and kicked her legs to propel herself forward,
waves washed her back again. She could see the rowboat
ahead in the water—but the swirling undertow twisted
her body sideways, tossing it back toward shore. She was
going nowhere—fast.

Almost there! You can do it, Jelly Bean!

Gideon's voice again—she must be hallucinating.

She flung out her aching arms, kicked her tired legs
like scissors. And then—yes!—she bumped against the
rowboat. She reached out, grabbed on, pulled herself up
to peer inside. Baby Helen lay on her back in about an
inch of cold water. Another wave broke against the boat
and sent a freezing, salty spray down over the silent baby.
She stared up at Clara in panic. She whimpered.

Alive!

They were both whimpering as Clara held tight to the
side of the boat and kicked desperately to propel it away

from the rocks. She could hear the bark of the seals now in the darkness, and she knew that they were very close. So were the rocks.

"Hang on now, Helen," gasped Clara, edging alongside the rowboat, never daring to release both hands at once, until finally she was at the rear of the small craft. "Your daddy is waiting for you." She started kicking again, trying to maintain a steady pace, trying to push the boat to shore.

She streaked through the water, reaching down for the figure trapped in seaweed, hauling him up onto the rocks...

Then a huge wave slammed into Clara and sucked her down, down into the deep darkness. She lost her grip on the rowboat as the water swirled over her head. The undertow tumbled her head-over-heels. She tried to hold her breath but felt she would burst if she couldn't fill her lungs with air...

She surfaced, gasping, her heart thudding hard, and dashed the water out of her eyes. She strained to see in the darkness. The rowboat was gone.

Had it capsized in the same wave that had nearly drowned her? Clara pivoted in the water, looking for the shore. She had lost her bearings. There! She could make out lantern lights bobbing on the beach. She pivoted the other way, treading water. *And there!* There was the rowboat—farther out now, still afloat.

But maybe full of water? Helen can't pull herself to sit up yet! She won't be able to get out of the water!

Clara struck out again for the boat. *One, two, three, four. One, two, three, four.* She counted her strokes as Gideon had when he was teaching her to swim.

Race you, Jelly Bean!

It was Gideon's voice again, egging her on. She kicked faster—and the extra spurt of energy brought her to the rowboat again. She grasped the side and peered in. Baby Helen lay in several inches of water, but her face was not submerged. Her eyes were closed now.

Was the baby still alive? Clara pushed the question out of her mind as she positioned herself behind the rowboat and started kicking again toward shore. The bobbing lights in the distance seemed so far now. It seemed she had been in the water forever...

Clara's strength was ebbing. She didn't see how she would get back to shore. She felt the undertow twisting beneath her and she fought against its pull.

Come on, Old Shoe, put a little muscle behind it!

She had to smile through her desperate tears. Gideon's voice in her head was as real as anything else on this nightmarish night, and she felt close to him, as if he were alive again, right there with her... And then suddenly the little boat seemed lighter in the water; suddenly it moved swiftly toward shore, as if the undertow had given up and gone away. Or—as if someone had surfaced next to her, someone stronger than she, who was swimming alongside, kicking mightily, giving a helping hand.

And then, finally, there in the water ahead, she could make out two dark shapes: Lucas Forrest and the deputy! They were paddling out to her aid and grabbed the boat as she approached. Together the three of them towed the rowboat back to the beach.

Clara collapsed on the sand as the men lifted Helen from the boat. She thought she would always hear the sound of waves in her head and taste salt on her tongue. She rested her head against the gritty sand.

Well done, Old Sock. You did it!

"W—we did it together," she stammered, and closed her eyes.

She felt rough wool being wrapped around her, and strong arms lifting her. She opened her eyes to find the senior policeman, who had remained on the beach, holding her. She was wrapped in his greatcoat but still felt so numb that she wondered if she would ever be warm again.

"Young lady, what a daring rescue!" exclaimed the policeman. "You are a much stronger swimmer than any of us, and thanks be to heaven for that!"

"You saved her!" Lucas Forrest wept openly. "Saved my daughter's life!"

Clara turned her head stiffly and saw Mr. Forrest at her side, cradling his baby. Behind him, Hattie Pitt and another woman who must be the baby's mother raced over the sand toward them. And Edgar was there, jumping up and down. Only Gideon was not there, and had he ever been? In her dreams she'd tried to do what no one had been able to do: save him. But the clamor of all the voices around her receded until she could hear only one voice now, the lusty yells of Baby Helen—Baby Helen, who was still very much alive.

Roseanna Forrest grabbed Clara and kissed her on the forehead. "My dear, you are our hero!"

Clara found she couldn't speak. Her body ached in every bone. She was chilled in every pore. But a great big smile spread across her face as she listened to the baby's cry, and little wings of warmth started fluttering deep inside her.

Chapter 15
OUT OF THE RUINS

Hattie Pitt rode back to the city in the Forrests' motorcar, and Edgar and Clara rode with the police. As they drove along the sandy road, rosy dawn lightened the sky. Two soldiers streaked past on horseback, blowing bugles. At the entrance to Golden Gate Park, a military band played triumphant marching music. Clara, huddled in the rumble seat with Edgar, watched in astonishment. Was all this fanfare to celebrate Baby Helen's rescue? How was it possible the news had traveled so fast?

The policeman driving their automobile stopped to speak to one of the soldiers, and the real reason for the celebration was made clear: the fires were out! At last, on this fourth morning since the earthquake, San Francisco was not in flames. The motorcar drove Clara and Edgar back to the boardinghouse, swerving to avoid hitting groups of cheering revelers in the street.

When they chugged up to Clara's house at last, the door burst open and Mother ran out onto the steps. A bandage wrapped her head like a turban, but this injury did not stop Mother from racing down the steps to the street.

"Clara, oh Clara!" Voice shaking, she clutched Clara to her breast. "We feared you were dead!"

Clara felt all the unshed tears of the fearful night welling up in her, and she wanted to crawl into Mother's lap as she used to do, bury her head against Mother's shoulder, and cry for joy that she was home again. But Mother led her inside to Father waiting in the hallway, holding out his arms. The lodgers were assembled behind him, relieved and curious.

Clara and Edgar were taken into the bedrooms and stripped of their wet garments. They were dressed in warm clothing and wrapped in dry blankets. Then they were settled into armchairs in the parlor and made to tell their stories over and over again. Humphrey snuggled up close to Clara and laid his shaggy head upon her knee. Mother poured them cups of hot coffee sweetened with tinned milk and plenty of sugar. The police officers took notes.

Clara was relieved to see Geoffrey Midgard and Hiram Stokes. The men explained that they had waited for the kidnappers at the tea garden but saw no one suspicious. They'd searched the entire park, looking for women in red dresses—but found no one who could help them. Mr. Stokes patted Clara's shoulder. "It took your more direct action to solve *this* case, my dear!"

"Oh, daughter," Father murmured, reaching out to stroke Clara's cheek. "To think I sent you out into the hands of such brutal men."

"But she escaped," Edgar reminded everyone.

"She saved herself," the policeman said. "*And* she saved the baby. It was the bravest rescue I have ever seen."

Father beamed, but Mother's eyes glazed as she stared at her daughter. "My own baby," she whispered. "You could so easily have been lost..."

Father reached out and gripped Mother's hand. "My dear." His voice was firm, comforting. "Our Clara is safe."

"But how could you risk it?" wept Mother, and Clara knew the question was as much for Father as it was for her. "After all we've already suffered?"

Clara reached for Mother's other hand, and the three of them sat there in the parlor, linked together for the first time since Gideon's death. "Baby Helen was nearly lost, too," Clara said. "I couldn't let that happen, could I?"

"If Clara *hadn't* tried to save the baby," added Father quietly, "she would have felt guilty for the rest of her life. And living each day wracked with the knowledge that you might have done something differently but didn't—" He hesitated, then raised his wife's hand to his lips and kissed it. "Believe me, that is no way to live. I am very proud of our daughter."

"Oh, so am I," whispered Mother. "So am I."

As words of praise washed over her, Clara snuggled deeper into her blankets. She could not stop shivering—not from cold now, but from fatigue, and from the certainty that she would never feel safe again. The Borden brothers were out there somewhere in the world, and that knowledge was a stone in the pit of her belly.

They got away, she thought desolately. *They'll kidnap somebody else sometime, in some other place.* Clara's belly clenched at the thought.

The policemen prepared to leave. "We still have work to do," the deputy said, as if he had read Clara's mind.

During the week that followed, the sound of hammers rang out through Clara's neighborhood as people boarded up broken windows and mended collapsed fences. Families moved back indoors, though cooking still had to take place out in the yards or streets; until the gas mains were repaired, it would not be safe to light stoves. All over San Francisco, relief crews were working to clear the rubble of fallen buildings, erect shelters for the thousands still homeless, and bury the dead. From all over the world, help was coming by train and boat in the form of food, water, clothing, household goods, and medical supplies.

Two days after the fires were out, the Hansen family left for Oakland, taking the Grissingers along with them.

Mrs. Hansen's brother had sent word that he would house them all until their own homes were rebuilt. The Wheeler sisters found to their delight that their home had not burned to the ground after all, though looters had made off with a good deal of the contents. Miss Chandler announced she would be leaving San Francisco for good, taking her piano-teaching talent north to Seattle. "People aren't going to be thinking about paying for extras like piano lessons around San Francisco anytime soon," she told Mother and Father. "Everything is changed now."

Everything felt changed to Clara, too, but for different reasons. At night she lay awake, hearing in every creak of the house a footstep, seeing in every shadow a revolver—aimed at her. When she did sleep, she dreamed of hiding from Sid and Herman Borden.

A happier change was in the air for Peggy DuBois and Hiram Stokes, who now, on the fifth afternoon since Clara's daring rescue, announced they planned to marry. They would like Clara to be their bridesmaid! They hoped to remain at the boardinghouse, however, until they could find a home of their own.

Clara smiled with pleasure and told them she would love to be a bridesmaid. Mr. Midgard and Mr. Granger made jokes about how roomy the boardinghouse would be with only the two of them left as lodgers.

"And me," Edgar piped up softly. "Don't forget me."

"Of course no one is forgetting you," Mother said.

"How could we forget the boy who has built us a real oven?" And then Mother decided that she would bake a special cake in the brick oven Edgar had constructed just that morning in the backyard. They would celebrate Clara's safe return and the end of the fires, and also, now, the betrothal. After so many days of gloom and fear, Clara found the cheerful bustle in the house a pleasant change.

She mixed a batter of flour, sugar, the last of the tinned milk, and eggs from the neighbors' chickens. A knock at the front door sent her hurrying down the hall-way. There on the step stood Emmeline. The two girls threw their arms around each other. "Come in!" cried Clara. "Oh, Emmy, I'm so glad to see you!"

"Such a lot has happened since we last saw each other," said Emmeline. Her family, she explained, had been visiting Emmeline's grandmother in Oakland when the quake hit—and of course they stayed on until word came that the fires were out in San Francisco. "We didn't know what we'd find when we came back," Emmeline told Clara. "We are so fortunate that we still have our house— and everything's still in it. But our school is gone—did you hear? And the cinedrome, too. But you—Clara, what is this I've been hearing about a kidnapping? All the neighborhood is talking! You must tell me everything."

"I will," Clara promised. "Stay for dinner, why don't you. It won't be fancy, but Mother has made plenty of fritters and barley soup, and we're even trying our hand at a cake in our new brick oven." She led her friend into the kitchen and introduced her to Edgar and the lodgers.

Edgar was pleased to meet Emmeline. "Want to taste this batter? Do you think it needs more sugar?"

Emmeline obliged, and there was much laughter from the lodgers as everyone offered to help taste the batter.

You should be happy, too! Clara told herself sternly, surveying the scene. But her heart felt heavy. The Borden brothers were still out there somewhere, she knew, and their evil lay like a weight inside her that even Emmeline's safe return could not banish. Humphrey sensed Clara's dread and pressed close. She closed her fingers in his thick fur and was glad for his reassuring bulk against her as she left Emmeline chatting in the kitchen and went out into the yard to tell Mother there would be one more for dinner.

"That's fine," Mother said. "We always have room for one more."

Edgar came out with the cake. He watched Mother check inside the brick oven. "Is it hot enough now, Mrs. Curfman?" he asked anxiously. "Shall I put the cake in to bake?"

"Feels mighty hot to me," she said cheerfully. "Put it inside and mind that you don't burn yourself. It should be ready by the time we finish our soup." She picked up the basket of fried corn fritters and headed for the house.

"Please bring the soup, Clara," she called from the doorway. "We're ready to eat."

Edgar lifted the metal lid of his oven and peered inside. "I'm going to wait out here until this cake is done."

"Fine—but don't keep peeking at it," Clara told him. "It'll never bake if you keep letting cold air in!" She wrapped her hands in potholders to lift the heavy pot of soup and walked up the ramp. Just as she entered the dining room, she heard the front doorbell ring. Mother excused herself and went to the door.

Clara set the pot on a sturdy trivet in the center of the table. *Always room for one more,* thought Clara, ladling soup into Emmeline's bowl. At least there was plenty of soup. As Clara moved around the table to serve Mr. Granger, she heard Mother's exclamation of delight and a murmur of voices ... And then there was Mother in the dining room doorway with a baby in her arms—*Helen!*—and Roseanna and Lucas Forrest close behind.

At the sight of the baby, a strange thing happened to Clara. All the courage she'd been showing since her escape from the Borden brothers deserted her. All the poise that her parents and the lodgers had admired since her return fell away. Her legs started shaking. The soup ladle sloshed back into the pot. She had to sit down in the nearest chair—Gideon's empty chair.

Baby Helen's face broke into a big smile. She reached out her arms to Clara. But Clara just sat staring at the baby, and her heart pounded like waves against Seal Rocks. An undertow seemed to be pulling at her again, pulling her into darkness. *They're still out there somewhere,* she thought. She dug her fingernails into her palms.

"We tried to telephone you, but, of course, all the lines are still down," Mr. Forrest said genially as he came into the dining room. "We didn't mean to interrupt your meal, but the ferries are completely without schedules — and it took us much longer to get here from Oakland than we'd expected."

Father rolled his chair away from the table to shake Lucas Forrest's hand. "You are most welcome to join us," he said. "Please come in and sit down."

Mother stroked the baby's smooth cheek. "Hello again, little one."

Baby Helen was passed around to all who wanted to hold her and marvel at her lucky escape from death. They exclaimed over the speed at which the dark fuzz atop her head was growing back into soft wisps. They admired her pretty lace dress.

Clara had to leave the room for a minute to pull herself together. She stood in the hallway and pushed her dark thoughts away. *Helen is fine. Everything is fine,* she told herself.

Chairs had been found for Lucas and Roseanna Forrest by the time Clara returned to the dining room. Mother was holding the baby again. Clara pulled over the stool from the sewing machine and sat at Mother's side so that

Gideon's chair could remain empty—as Mother liked it.

"We are full of news," Mr. Forrest began. "First of all, we are interviewing for a new nanny for Helen. So if you know of anyone who might like the position, please send her to us. Hattie and her no-good boyfriend have run off together—probably to Alaska."

"I thought Hattie might be in jail," Clara said quietly.

"Well, maybe she should be. But we didn't press charges," replied Mr. Forrest.

"She always took good care of Helen," his wife hastened to explain. "And I do believe she never meant for our daughter to be put into danger. She told us she had no idea of the kidnapping scheme until the Borden brothers were pointing a revolver at her—and I believed her."

"We have only ever heard Hattie's account of the kidnapping," Mother said. "Please do tell us your story."

Mr. and Mrs. Forrest exchanged a troubled glance. "It's still painful to talk about," Mr. Forrest said. "But of course you must know all the details." And everyone listened eagerly, sipping soup, as Lucas Forrest told his tale.

He and his wife had been guests of the Plumsteads when the earthquake hit. They were all lucky to escape safely moments before the mansion collapsed. Panicked, Lucas and Roseanna were desperate to get home to their baby in Oakland, so they left the Plumsteads and their Nob Hill neighbors to fight the oncoming fire and headed straight for the ferry building.

Mrs. Forrest put her hand to her mouth to stifle a laugh. "Tell them about Caruso!" she interrupted.

Mr. Forrest smiled. "Enrico Caruso, the famous tenor we had seen at the opera the night before the quake, was making a scene at the ferry! He was demanding to be taken away from this 'Godforsaken city' ahead of everyone else. 'Don't you know who I am?' he kept shouting importantly, but no one cared. We were ahead of him in line for the ferry when he came pushing past us, roaring that he had sung for kings and presidents! The ferry operator yelled at him, 'Well, go ahead, then, if you're so famous—SING!'"

The Curfmans and the lodgers laughed.

"And Caruso sang," Mrs. Forrest continued. "He stood right there and belted out songs from *Carmen*. So they let him on the ferry and he sang the whole way to Oakland."

Mr. Forrest shook his head. "I'm afraid we didn't appreciate the honor. All we could think about was getting home to Helen. It took ages to get to our house—Oakland is also badly damaged. When we finally arrived, we were so grateful to be among the fortunate whose houses were still standing. But—"

"But there was no sign of Helen!" cried Mrs. Forrest. "Our housekeeper said she'd seen Hattie and the baby heading for the ferry to San Francisco on Tuesday afternoon and thought she was bringing Helen over to stay with us at the Plumsteads'. When we heard this, we feared

both Helen and Hattie had been killed in the quake."
She cast a tender glance at her daughter, who sat happily
on Mother's lap. "We never for a moment imagined she'd
been kidnapped..."

Mrs. Forrest's voice trailed off, but her husband
resumed their account. "We paid a man to take us back
to San Francisco in his sailboat, though he insisted we
were mad to return. But we needed to post notices that
Helen was missing. We stayed with the Plumsteads in
Golden Gate Park so that we could search day and night."

Mrs. Forrest's voice rose in agitation. "The next thing
we knew, a ransom note had been slipped under the front
door of our house in the dead of night! Our housekeeper
notified the police, who then came to the park to alert us.
As you can imagine, we were beside ourselves. And of
course you know the rest of the story."

"But perhaps they don't, dear," Mr. Forrest said.
"Because our most important news is some we wanted
to bring you ourselves, before the police stop by to tell
you. They sent word to us only this morning that the
Borden brothers have been found."

Clara's mouth grew dry. She licked her lips.

"As they tried to flee that awful night, their boat was
dashed on the rocks and sank. Their accomplices—two
sailors who may not even have known what the brothers
were up to—drowned, poor things. The Borden brothers
tried to swim to shore, but Sid didn't make it. He drowned

just beyond Seal Rocks, and his body washed ashore. Herman Borden made it to land but was arrested before he got himself dried off. He's on his way to prison now."

Clara felt as if a choking noose around her neck had been cut free. She took a deep breath and tried to feel compassion for Sid's death and Herman's capture, but all she really felt was gladness. They deserved whatever they got, she believed. And now they would not be able to hurt anyone else, ever again.

She reached over and lifted Helen from Mother's arms. "Little one," she whispered. "Now we are truly safe."

"Our Helen is alive because of you, Clara." Mrs. Forrest's voice trembled. "We have no words to thank you enough. You have our eternal gratitude."

Clara pressed her face against Helen's fuzzy head and could not answer. Father and Mother were beaming across the table at each other.

"We know there's nothing we can do to thank Clara adequately—but we'd like to try," Mr. Forrest added, looking down the table at Father. "My wife attended Mills College, the women's college over in Oakland, where her own father is a professor. And it would be our greatest honor to see Clara continue her education there someday. Her full tuition would be taken care of, of course."

"Oh, my, we couldn't accept such a gift!" exclaimed Father.

"Please, Mr. Curfman, you must let us do this," said

Mrs. Forrest gently. "Without Clara, our Helen would be dead. Can you imagine the pain of losing a child?" She shuddered.

Several of the lodgers cleared their throats uncomfortably.

Mother closed her eyes. "Yes," she whispered. "Yes, we can."

Mrs. Forrest glanced around the table, then hurriedly continued. "Anyway, we think of Clara now as one of our own family, and all the young ladies in our family go to Mills College!"

"Unless, of course, Clara would prefer to go to college elsewhere—" amended Mr. Forrest.

"Oh no," said Clara. "Mills College would be lovely. Oh, thank you, Mr. and Mrs. Forrest! Going to college has been one of my fondest dreams!"

Emmeline spoke up. "It's true—Clara loves school—she wants to be a teacher. I daresay she's the only one in our class who is sad that the school has burned down."

Everyone joined in the laughter. Then the back door slammed and Edgar came in at last, carrying the cake. "It's finally ready!" he cried, then stopped and looked at the Forrests in surprise. "Oh! I surely hope there will be enough to go around!"

Mother smiled at Edgar. "I'm sure there will be. But first, you need some supper yourself." She ladled out a bowl of soup, and then hesitated a moment, looking

around the table, before she passed the bowl down to
Father at the other end. Clara held her breath as Father
set the bowl at the only free place: Gideon's place. Clara
looked up in time to see Father and Mother exchange a
long look, the sort of wordless conversation they used to
have before the accident. Clara smiled to see it. Then
Father touched the back of Gideon's chair.

"Go on, Edgar," Clara said quickly before Mother
could change her mind. "Hurry, before your soup is cold.
Sit down!"

Edgar, taking his place at the table, flashed a smile.
"Don't mind if I do," he said. "Old Sock."

Old Sock?

Had Edgar really spoken—or had she imagined
those words?

Maybe it doesn't matter, Clara thought, kissing the
top of Helen's head. Here she was, sitting in a room
full of people—some whom she'd known before the
quake, some whom she'd met only because of the
disaster. It was easy to imagine that Gideon was here
with them, too. He would always be with her, she felt
sure. The city lay in ruins, yet her own family felt less
damaged now, after the quake. She wasn't quite sure
how it had happened, but she looked over at Mother,
then at Father, and was certain it had. And now there
was Edgar. And the promise of college. Clara hugged
Baby Helen. Who would have thought in a million years

that so much could change in such a very short time?

"Clara," Mother said briskly, interrupting Clara's reverie. "Will you please clear the table, dear? And bring in plates for cake?"

Some things, of course, would never change. Not in a million years.

A Peek into
the Past

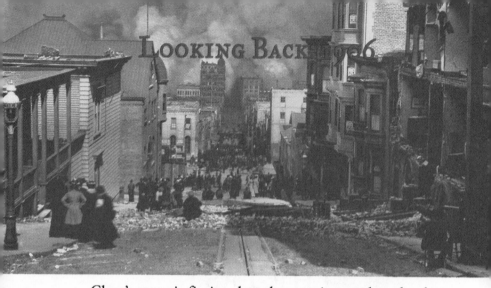

Clara's story is fiction, but the massive earthquake that rocked San Francisco on April 18, 1906, really happened. The quake—caused by shifts in the earth miles below the surface—struck at 5:12 A.M. and created one of the worst disasters in United States history. Hundreds of buildings collapsed, gas mains broke, and fires spread swiftly, engulfing the city center. More than six square miles were reduced to rubble and ash, and over 3,000 people were killed. Many towns and villages were damaged in the earthquake, but only San Francisco was ravaged by fire.

Fires raged for three days and three nights. Fire Chief Dennis Sullivan died after his house collapsed, leaving no one in charge of the fire-fighting effort. Mansions burned as well as slums, and many people were separated from their families. Notices were tacked up all over town, and especially at the tent cities in Golden Gate Park, to help people reunite with loved ones.

EXTRA THE DAILY NEWS EXTRA

HUNDREDS DEAD!

Fire Follows Earthquake, Laying Downtown
Section in Ruins--City Seems Doomed
For Lack of Water

MISSING

Mrs. Bessie O. Steele
Age 33, dark hair, brown eyes, 5 ft. 3 in.
weight 135; slender

Helen Steele
6 years old, brown eyes

Donald Steele
3 years old, blue eyes

Mrs. H. O. Wheeler
Age 55, iron gray hair, eyes gray, 5 ft. 2 in.
heavy build, weight 150 lbs.

Were supposed to be stopping at

Rex Hotel, 242 Turk St.

The tent cities were
organized by the army,
following orders from
President Theodore Roosevelt.
Over 250,000 people were homeless, and more than 100,000 of them
lived for months in the park, standing in long lines at relief
stations for free food, water, and clothing and sleeping in
temporary shelters. Across the bay, residents of Oakland
welcomed the refugees escaping San Francisco
by ferry. Mills College sheltered many former
students, as well as professors and their families.
People all over America sent help by train and
boat. They sent clothes and food, medical
supplies, tents, and blankets—all desperately
needed by suffering San Franciscans.

Out of the chaos came accounts of brave rescue
and lucky escape. There was the baby, born at home
just as the earthquake caused the house to sink
below street level, sealing off the doors.
The newborn and her mother
were rescued by two boys who
climbed through a window as
the fire swept toward them.
Another girl was carried
to safety by her father—
straight out of their attic
window, which had
dropped to street level!

*Homes shaken from their
foundations by the quake*

Cooking outside after the quake

After the fires were out, the fear of fire remained. For months after the quake, even families like the Curfmans, whose homes were still standing, had to cook outdoors. No one was allowed to light a stove until the gas mains and electric lines had been repaired and an inspector had declared that cooking indoors would be safe again. In many cases, this permission did not come for nine months after the quake! At first, people made do with campfires, but as time passed, they moved their cookstoves outside or built outdoor ovens. Some people even built rustic kitchen shacks around their ovens.

Although travel in the city was difficult because of the piles of rubble from collapsed buildings, some enterprising restaurant owners hung signboards advertising their fare and set up tables and chairs in the street for customers. The business district had been totally demolished, but grocers, bakers, and seamstresses opened temporary shops on street corners.

It was months before schools were rebuilt, and although some teachers tried to hold classes outdoors, most children did not return to school until September because they stayed home to

Children at class under a makeshift tent

help their families. People shared space for worship services until their synagogues and churches could be rebuilt. Almost every bank had burned, but some businessmen set up makeshift counters and loaned people money to rebuild their houses.

Enrico Caruso, the great opera singer who fled San Francisco after the quake, really did sing on his ferry passage to Oakland. He vowed he would never return to San Francisco, and he never did. But even if he had, concert halls, museums, art galleries, and hotels were not rebuilt for several years. People had more pressing matters to worry about.

As San Francisco pulled itself out of the wreckage, however, families started to enjoy whatever leisure activities were still available in their desolate, charred city. The

Opera star Enrico Caruso

Sutro Baths and Cliff House were popular destinations both before and after the earthquake. Neither was badly damaged in the quake, although an early newspaper account that Clara might have read reported that Cliff House had toppled into the sea.

Cliff House, overlooking Seal Rocks, in the early 1900s

Cliff House was first built in 1856, of lumber salvaged from a ship wrecked on the cliffs below. Cliff House burned and was rebuilt several times, and in 1896 a man named Adolph Sutro bought the property. He had made his fortune mining silver and gold and later became mayor of San Francisco. He erected a huge, eight-story Cliff House that resembled a French chateau and opened it to the public. People enjoyed the fine food and dancing, the art galleries and musical events—and also, of course, the stunning views of the ocean, Seal Rocks, and the towering cliffs. Today, there are busy roads running through bustling neighbor-

hoods straight from Golden Gate Park down to the ocean, but in 1906 Clara would have driven across sand dunes and scrub brush to reach Cliff House. Sutro's beautiful Cliff House burned completely in 1907, a year after the earthquake.

The nearby swimming baths also were built by Adolph Sutro. The sprawling pavilion resembled a crystal palace, and people came from all around to rent suits and swim, play on the slides and trapezes, and leap from springboards into water tanks filled by the tides. In 1906, up to 25,000 people came daily, for a

fee of 25 cents. The building was demolished in 1966,
and today only ruins remain on the site, right at the edge
of Ocean Beach.

    Ocean Beach is not a place for swimmers because of the
deadly riptide and unpredictable currents that still, all too
often, sweep people to their deaths. Clara's father's steamship
met its end on the treacherous rocks, which were the scene
of more than 50 shipwrecks between 1850 and
1936. In the days before foghorns, ship
captains listened for the loud barks of
sea lions on Seal Rocks to guide them
between the dangerous headlands of the
Golden Gate channel.

    People who lived through the San Francisco earthquake
of 1906 never forgot the suffering, fires, and destruction it
caused—nor the extraordinary lengths some San Franciscans
went to to help one another. The survivors learned that
disaster can bring people together even as the world seems
to be in chaos. Then, as now, it is in such times of trouble
that ordinary people like Clara often find the strength to
take matters into their own hands and emerge as heroes.

*Thanks to the courage
and hard work of thou-
sands of San Franciscans,
the city recovered from
the earthquake of 1906.
Today, beautiful homes
and gleaming skyscrapers
stand where the quake
once left acres of rubble
and ashes.*

AUTHOR'S NOTE

In researching this story, I read many moving and fascinating accounts of the 1906 earthquake and fire. As I wrote Clara's fictional adventure, I included historical details, events, and people I found especially interesting. For instance:

The notices Clara reads in Golden Gate Park were real ones posted by desperate family members in search of lost loved ones after the quake.

The jujubes that Edgar offers Clara came from Blum's Candy Store, a real shop that was dynamited as part of the firebreak. Before the shop was destroyed, police officers really did offer children the chance to run in and take as many sweets as they could carry.

The singer Enrico Caruso really did sing songs from *Carmen* as the ferry carried him away from the burning city. General Funston and Fire Chief Sullivan were real people, too.

And although the Borden brothers are fictional, criminals did try get-rich-quick schemes to take advantage of people during the chaotic aftermath of the earthquake.

Today San Francisco is a shining city built on hills and edged by ocean and bay. It is home to millions of people who wouldn't want to live anywhere else. But occasional earth movements are uncomfortable reminders of the region's past—and motivation to build carefully on this unsettled edge of earth.

Readers who want to learn more about the 1906 earthquake and fire will enjoy reading *If You Lived at the Time of the Great San Francisco Earthquake* by Ellen Levine, *Earthquake at Dawn* by Kristiana Gregory, *The Earth Shook, The Sky Burned* by William Bronson, and *Disaster* by Dan Curzman.

ABOUT THE AUTHOR

Kathryn Reiss grew up in Ohio. When she wasn't dreaming of being transported back to the nineteenth century, she had her nose in a book—usually a mystery. When she couldn't find anything the slightest bit eerie or criminal happening in her neighborhood, she started writing stories about mysteries she *wished* she would uncover.

Now she lives with her husband, three children, two cats, and dog in a 130-year-old house in northern California, not far from San Francisco. She has felt several small earthquakes—and one big one—but is still waiting to find a baby in a basket on her doorstep.

Her previous novels have won many awards. The titles are *Riddle of the Prairie Bride, Paint by Magic, Time Windows, Pale Phoenix, The Glass House People, Dreadful Sorry, PaperQuake*, and the "Ghost in the Dollhouse" trilogy. She teaches writing at Mills College.

Free catalogue!

Welcome to a world that's all yours—because it's filled with the things girls love! Beautiful dolls that capture your heart. Books that send your imagination soaring. And games and pastimes that make being a girl great!

For your free American Girl® catalogue, return this postcard, call 1-800-845-0005, or visit our Web site at americangirl.com.

Send me a catalogue:

_____   ___/___/___
Name   Girl's birth date

_____
Address

_____
City   State   Zip

_____
E-mail   *Fill in to receive updates and Web-exclusive offers.*

(_____)_____
Phone   ❏ Home ❏ Work

_____
Parent's signature   12583i

Send my friend a catalogue:

_____
Name

_____
Address

_____
City   State   Zip

                                    12591i

Try it risk-free!

American Girl® magazine is especially for girls 8 and up. Send for your preview issue today! Mail this card to receive a risk-free preview issue and start your one-year subscription. For just $19.95, you'll receive 6 bimonthly issues in all! If you don't love it right away, just write "cancel" on the invoice and return it to us. The preview issue is yours to keep, free!

Send bill to: (please print)

_____
Adult's name

_____
Address

_____
City   State   Zip

_____
Adult's signature

Send magazine to: (please print)

_____   ___/___/___
Girl's name   Birth date

_____
Address

_____
City   State   Zip

American Girl ®
PO BOX 620497
MIDDLETON WI 53562-0497

BUSINESS REPLY MAIL
FIRST-CLASS MAIL   PERMIT NO. 190   BOONE IA

POSTAGE WILL BE PAID BY ADDRESSEE

American Girl ®
PO BOX 37311
BOONE IA 50037-2311